Killer's Crew

(A DI Shona McKenzie Mystery)

Wendy H. Jones

Published by Scott and Lawson

Copyright © Wendy H. Jones, 2015

www.wendyhjones.com

Cover Design by Cathy Helms of Avalon Graphics LLC

ISBN: 978-0-9945657-0-7

DEDICATION

To Elizabeth and Mandy for all their support to help bring this book to fruition.

ACKNOWLEDGMENTS

I would like to thank the following people who have helped me in so many ways.

Elizabeth Kwasnik for her tireless work with editing.

Karen Wilson of Ginger Snap Images, Dundee for the professional author photographs.

Nathan Gevers for all his hard work and enthusiasm building the website for my books.

Police Scotland for their patience in answering myriad questions about the nuts and bolts of policing. Particular thanks must go to my local police sergeant who has never failed to answer any of my questions with good humour and has supported me in my endeavour.

.

1

The body twisted slowly in the soft sough of a gentle Scottish breeze. Swinging high above the masts of the old sailing ship, a macabre addition to an otherwise peaceful, early morning scene. The wooden decks of this ship had seen many deaths but not one such as this malevolent presence, brooding and dark. It marked a turning point in history, one from which there would be no return. From this point onwards the ship would be known, not for its heroic past, but for its evil present.

The ship lay like a lone sentinel, permanently moored in an insignificant dock. Surrounded by the gloomy swell of shallow water enclosed by grey concrete. A once proud denizen of the seas, now tamed and caged. Serving only as an aid to remember what had been. Humbled and brought to man's bidding yet displaying its glorious heritage and refusing to bow.

The sounds of creaking timbers, from the thick oak hull, were gently picked up and carried away on the light breeze. They whispered of shadowy deeds, of murder known only to one living soul. The other participant would tell no more tales. Not in this life anyway.

The black-cloaked figure studied their handiwork. Satisfied, they slipped quietly away. The soft lapping of the water sang a quiet chorus accompanying it on its way. Light and dark came together in one malevolent scene. The figure hurried along the banks of the river and slipped into a tangle of ancient unlit streets. Darkness enfolded the fleeing figure in its grasp. With silent footsteps it vanished from sight.

Death once more stalked the streets of this ancient city, claiming the night for its own.

Detective Inspector Shona McKenzie's long legs made short work of the walk leading to the entrance to the crime scene. It was a bustling hive of activity. Coppers had surrounded the area with miles of crime scene tape but still a throng of Jock Public jostled and pushed to get a better view. There were cell phones aplenty recording every little detail. Fortunately, the main attraction was too far away to be photographed clearly. Each eager shouted voice was more strident than the last. Shona whipped around and shouted above the bedlam, "Shut up the lot of you." Her voice was darted into the middle of the fray and hung there. Ineffectual.

A scruffy, black and white mongrel broke loose from its owner's grasp and, lead trailing, lunged under the tape. A couple of burly uniformed Bobbies hurtled off in hot pursuit.

"You have got to be kidding me? Get that mutt out of my crime scene."

The police Official Licensed Search Advisor or POLSA just rolled his eyes. After a few years of Shona being around *his* crime scenes nothing surprised him. "Feel free to go in and take a look, Ma'am." He allowed Shona to think she owned the scene. Only he knew better.

Shona stared at the body hanging from the metal structure, stark against the background of the rigging and the bright blue sky. The RRS Discovery had discovered something new that morning. Its first death since its Antarctic voyage in 1901.

The repetitive clang of metal on metal made her

brain shudder. Riverfront regeneration meant building sites aplenty and constant background music complements of heavy metal pile drivers. "What exactly is that he's swinging from?" she shouted.

"Camera dolly."

"Nina Chakrabarti, how exactly do you know that?"

"I was an extra on a few episodes of Taggart. I hooked up with a cameraman."

Shona shook her head at another tale of her sergeant's numerous conquests. Despite also being bosom buddies with Nina it was the first she'd heard of any acting in her background.

"It's a funny place to hang yourself," said Jason Roberts, one of the team's PCs.

"It would take some doing," said Shona.

"I would've changed my mind before I got there."

"The master of the daft statement as always, Roy. Why don't you try thinking before you speak?"

"Sorry, Ma'am." His grin belied his words.

"That's some piece of equipment," said Shona. "Iain, find out from the POLSA when we can get up close and personal with it."

Iain Barrow scurried to do her bidding. The quicker this task was over, the quicker he could get on with his real job. Cataloguing the crime scene. Fingerprints waited.

The rest of them stared, mesmerised by the swinging body.

"It's almost hypnotic," said Abigail.

Despite secretly agreeing, Shona said, "Sergeant Lau, you may want to rephrase that. The poor man deserves respect."

Iain returned with good news. The POLSA had declared the area open to them.

Grabbing white coveralls, they struggled into them.

"Are these getting smaller? They're a tad on the tight side." Jason had his right leg in the coveralls. He toppled as he tried to force his left leg in beside its partner.

"You need to give up having a wee swallie." Shona heaved him up. "Drinking so many pints isn't good for you."

She'd taken no more than one confident step toward the scene when a man who could double as a Viking accosted her. He had a brace of bouncers with him, dressed in the obligatory dark suits with matching sunglasses. Even the wires of their earpieces blended in. A pair of walking clichés in fact.

"Get away from my film scene. This has taken weeks to set up. You'll ruin it."

"There's a dead body swinging from the jib. Don't you think it's already ruined? Unless you put it there of course."

The Viking jerked his head up. "What... What... What's that doing there?"

"If you let us get on we might be able to find out."

The bouncers took one step forward.

Shona mirrored them and said, "Tell hoods one and two here if they don't leave my crime scene right now they'll be accompanied by the blue flashing light brigade."

"Dennis and James you can go."

After a bit of posturing from the hoods and prompting from Shona's team the pair left them to it.

"You can't go in there. It's ready for filming." The Viking's eyes had returned to the slowly swinging corpse.

"With all due respect Mr....?"

"Lovelady. Xavier Lovelady."

"Mr Lovelady, this is now a crime scene not your

film set."

"Do you know how much this is costing me?"

"A lot more if you stand here nattering. Now please move aside. One of my officers would like to ask you some questions." She nodded to Abigail who came at a trot. "Your first question should be, why is Mr Lovelady traipsing his size nines around my crime scene?"

A look of disdain took up position on the Viking's face. "My feet are a size fourteen."

"Whatever." Her gaze didn't veer from Abigail. "Take Roy with you," she said, keeping her voice low, "Mr Viking here might give you a bit of trouble."

The protesting Lovelady was dragged off in the direction of the Discovery café, where the POLSA had set up their HQ.

The remainder of the team approached the camera dolly.

It was slow progress. They searched the area inch by painful inch. This being a film set there were at least a couple of hundred people who were legally allowed to traipse around the area. This made it difficult to pin down the one who was there for nefarious reasons.

They stopped at the bottom and craned their neck to get a better view.

"How do we get up there?" asked Iain. "It's a long way to be clambering."

"I assume it goes up and down electronically."

"You assume rightly young lady."

Shona whirled around. A twinkling-eyed gnome, in a fuschia pink pullover, was treading on her crime scene. This was a cue for fireworks.

"How did you get in here? You can leave right now." With a wave of her arm she indicated to Jason that he should assist the man on his way.

Jason put one hand on the man's arm and that was his undoing. He found himself flat on his back. Before the others could react the gnome said, "I'm the cameraman. You'll want me to lower the dolly."

It turned out that the POLSA had ushered the man through.

"If you'd been escorted then there would have been no misunderstanding." Not that Shona was going to take that up with the POLSA. His word was law when it came to crime scenes. She wasn't going to take it up with the gnome either. She rather fancied staying upright.

"Jason, please don't tell me you're injured?"

"Bit of a sore arm but chirpy otherwise."

"Good. Any trips to A&E during this case and I'm dumping you in a chair and never letting you out again. Got it?"

"Never been more got in my life."

"Iain, before Mr—" She stopped and raised a quizzical eyebrow towards he gnome.

"Tasker, but call me Ernie."

"—Ernie lowers the crane can you get some photos. Surely one of those super expensive lenses must do close-ups?"

"Of course they do, Ma'am." His hands were busy clicking on a lens the size of the Eiffel Tower. A power lens on steroids it could take a picture of a nut on the top of the arm and make it look crisp.

While Iain's fingers were busy clicking, Shona took the opportunity to speak to Ernie. She pulled her pink sunglasses out of her voluminous leather handbag and put them on. The sunlight coupled with the sweater had her head banging like a snare drum during a performance of Bolero.

"What's going on here Ernie?"

7

Anyone living in Dundee and its environs already knew the answer to that question. You would have had to be in cold storage to have missed it. However, the horse's mouth might elicit more information than *The Dundee Courier*. In fact anything would elicit more information than the local press.

"You'll need to be a bit more specific young lady. Do you mean the rather unfortunate corpse, or what our esteemed director and crew are doing?"

Shona shoved her hands in the pocket of her dress in an attempt to stop them wrapping around the gnome's scrawny neck. She took a couple of deep breaths and said, "The filming. The setup here. Plus, we don't know if it's a corpse or a dummy yet. No speculating."

Ernie straightened up to his full height, which still found him several inches shorter than Shona. Her posture said she'd speculate about his death if he didn't hurry up.

"My dear girl, have you not heard we are filming a blockbuster movie about the life of Captain Robert Falcon Scott, one of the greatest explorers of all time?"

He might have been a jolly nice chap, and all round good egg, but that's taking adulation a bit far thought Shona. *A trip to the Antarctic and back in the nineteen hundreds doesn't exactly compare with discovering the Indies.*

"I had heard something about it. Can you give me a few more details?"

It wasn't long before her glazed look indicated she regretted asking. After having listened for about seven minutes, or thereabouts, she said, "Fascinating as this is Ernie, could you tell us more about the filming and less about the script?"

"How can you not be interested in Robert Falcon Scott?"

"I'm interested in everything about him but perhaps later. I've an alleged body literally swinging in the wind. I'd rather like to solve the case before they're doing movies about our lives."

"What would you like to know dear lady?"

Biting back a sigh Shona said, "How would they get the body up there?" *It was better to keep things simple with this one,* she thought.

"In some ways it is the easiest thing in the world. In others impossible."

She gave into the inevitable and decided to mirror his language. It might speed the process up.

"Would you care to elaborate, Ernie?"

"It is a simple matter of lowering the dolly, attaching the rope and the body and then raising it again."

Shona, her right foot tapping out the Dashing White Sergeant, said, "And the impossible part?"

"The only person with a key to the dolly is me."

"Sounds like you're the killer then."

The bristling and straightening made a reappearance. "Indeed I am not. How dare you imply such a thing?"

"It wasn't so much of an implication as a statement of fact."

"If you think I did this then arrest me. Otherwise I am leaving."

"Don't tempt me." She turned round. "Roy, keep an eye on Ernie here. Take a statement."

With an imperious wave of the arm Roy invited the gnome to join him in the Discovery Cafe.

As they disappeared off Shona shouted, "Oi. Leave the keys for the jib behind."

"That is an important piece of equipment, you can't operate it." His level of outrage was in direct proportion to the generosity of the saliva that sprayed from his mouth.

"Give my Constable a lesson. He's a clever lad, he'll work it out." With a flick of her head she dragged Iain over.

"Before you go, could whoever's swinging up there have done it themselves?"

"Even more impossible. The operator keeps his or her finger on the button until it reaches the correct angle."

Not suicide then. They had themselves a murder.

As they walked away she could hear Roy saying. "I was just wondering. Are there any nuns or vicars in the movie?"

"Of course not you foolish boy. It's a tale of adventure in the frozen wastes not a romp through the Vatican."

Shona couldn't help thinking the foolish boy had a point. Her cases usually seemed to be awash with nuns and vicars. Hopefully there would be nary a one in this case.

3

With all the mosquito-like luvvies gone, Shona turned once more to the swaying body. She took one step forward and found herself face down, choking on dust and listening to muffled laughter.

She coughed as choking dust billowed around her, struggled to her knees and said, "Ernie, if you've floored me I swear I will lock you up for a million years."

A strong hand grasped her arm and yanked her upright. "Whoever Ernie is he's missing in action."

The words were a whispered caress in her ear. She whirled round, lifted her arms towards him then forced them down against her sides.

"Douglas." Her smile dialled up the sunlight by a million watts. The Procurator Fiscal had arrived. Her delight had less to do with the case and more to do with him being her boyfriend. Who doesn't like to see their fella on a sunny day. Most people's trysts involve food or a walk along the beach. Hers usually had a dead body along as an escort.

"Take a look down. You'll see what attacked you." His voice still held a hint of laughter, his eyes full of it.

Her head snapped downwards as directed, and took in a thick rope of cables snaking their way across the dockside.

"You'd think my biggest worry would be gun-toting thugs. Now I've murderous cables thrown into the mix."

"You could try watching where you're going."

She stepped over the offending cable and pointed upwards. "My eyes were heavenward taking in our chum here."

Looking up Douglas squinted against the sunlight. "I take it the body's real?"

"Looks like. Iain will have it lowered in a jiffy and we can take a butcher's."

The body was indeed real. Closer proximity showed it to be a man of about thirty with a shock of spiky vibrant ginger hair and an unkempt beard. He was dressed as a sailor. Shona was willing to guess the dress was early twentieth century. Easy given the movie's time period.

"Either this corpse is part of the film crew or it's some sort of kinky sex game gone wrong."

"Knowing your reputation it'll be both o' them." Peter Johnston, sergeant and stalwart of the team, had sidled up behind them.

"Nice of you to join us, Peter. Walk over the Tay Bridge from Tayport did you?"

"The wife's in Wick for a couple of weeks and the car's gone wi' her. Had to get the bus."

"Seriously! I'm running an investigation to the vagaries of the local bus services."

"Afraid so, Ma'am. Had to get the number 42 to Dundee, then the number 29 takes you to Bell Street."

"And the number 666 takes you straight to hell, which is where you'll be dispatched if you don't get some work done." Her shoulders slumped. "One of us will pick you up in future."

"A taxi service? That's just the job."

"Abuse it and you're moving to traffic."

The massive grin said Peter wasn't too worried about the threat. The regularity of its use had the team inoculated against it. "At least I'd get a lift to work."

They were interrupted by a cyclone of grey dust from which appeared a pink and green whirlwind. The police surgeon.

"Whitney. To what do we owe the pleasure?"

Whitney Williams usually plied her trade in Perthshire.

"Larry's retired. I interviewed and got the gig so you're stuck with me now."

"How did I not know that?"

A loud snort came from Peter's direction. "Probably because you throw most o' your memos in the bin, Ma'am."

"Traffic, Peter."

Whilst this pleasant exchange was taking place, Whitney was busy examining the body.

She poked, prodded, checked and measured, then said, "This one was alive when he was hanged. The first death by hanging in Scotland since Henry John Burnett in Aberdeen in 1963. First in Dundee since 1868."

"You're a mine of information Whitney. Larry barely said a word." Shona raised an admiring eyebrow.

Whitney was nowhere near to hear the compliment. The whirlwind was disappearing in the direction of Dundee City Centre.

As she donned white coveralls Shona said, "I think I might die of heat exhaustion. I should go au naturel inside them."

"Shona, much as I would love to see that, it may be too much information for the rest of the world," said Douglas.

The heat in his voice made Shona come over all hot and helpless. The rest of the world, in the shape of Shona's team, was too busy dragging on coveralls to pay much attention. Grumbling could be heard coming from Peter's direction.

"How come we're ordering small now? Yir average bobby disnae fit them."

Ignoring his moaning as per, Shona approached the body. She stepped past Iain and his camera and peered at the corpse. Wide staring eyes gazed at her from a dusky face atop an unnaturally elongated neck. Despite the rope cutting into his neck, ligature marks could clearly be seen. Add to that he had a couple of broken legs. This was apparent from the bones sticking through the legs of the sailor's bell-bottom trousers. There was also a lot of blood on the trousers and what looked like fragments of bone. The broken bones might be theatrical make-up produced for some other purpose of course. Mary, the pathologist, would be able to give a definitive. The knuckles of both hands were also covered in bruises and scraped.

The noose was made of rope, thin and yet strong. Shona counted thirteen coils. The precise number for a perfect hangman's noose. It was also positioned next to the left ear. Whoever tied this knew what they were doing.

In the meantime, "Sergeant Chakrabarti when you're finished loafing, go find our man Loveless—"

"Lovelady, Ma'am." Nina, dressed in coveralls and a pair of Jimmy Choo's, was leaning against the railing at the side of the River Tay.

"—Whatever. Go find him and ask if he's missing any crewmembers. Change your shoes whilst you're at it. What gives you the impression high heels are perfect for a crime scene?"

"Nothing else with me."

"I swear if you don't appear in some different footwear you'll be wearing running shoes from the boot of my car. "

The hurried clicking of high heels on cement dock signified Nina had taken in the urgency of the command.

Shona watched her go, wondering how the girl could walk in those shoes. Especially since she was now walking on cobbles. It was always a matter of wonder to Shona how Nina could perform her duties so brilliantly in heels that a circus performer would consider to be unwise. Yet she did.

4

Roy and Abigail were having a difficult time with Xavier Lovelady. Abigail let Roy take the lead. He was thinking of taking his Sergeant exams and needed the experience. The man's whiney, pretentious voice instantly poked holes in Roy's brain. If Xavier had been interested in anyone but himself he would have taken in Roy's narrowing eyes and fighter's stance. This would be his cue to shut up. Roy's hands twitched as he stuffed them in the pockets of his chinos. Smacking witnesses in the face tended to slow up an investigation. Being one detective short did that. *I didn't join the force to listen to pontificating jumped up luvvies.*

The three things he took from the blah, blah, blah, were

1. Xavier thought the body was a dummy set up to ruin his perfect movie schedule.

2. Everyone was jealous of Xavier and his success.

3. Xavier didn't have time for any of this and the police ought to wrap things up and shove off.

In fact it was the world according to Xavier. Roy was beginning to think that not a judge in the land would find him guilty if he rid the world of the man. They'd probably promote him.

"Mr Lovelady, for heavens sake, shut it and let me ask some questions."

"You can't—"

"Yes I can. I can't do my job for all the crap that's coming out of your mouth. So shut up and only speak to answer my questions."

The Viking made to stand up. Jason, who was

standing nearby, stepped in. He encouraged Xavier to sit back down. This involved a large hand to the shoulder. Jason 'Soldier Boy' Roberts learned a trick or two in the army.

"Ask your questions Roy, I'll keep Jimmy here on the straight and narrow 'til you're finished."

"Have you any idea who that might be swinging from the jib?"

"Are you deaf? I said it's a dummy."

Roy's trigger finger itched but he kept it civil. "How many people have access to the area?"

"How would I know you stupid boy? The whole of Scotland could have a key."

"That's it. I've had just about enough of you. One more stupid statement out of your fu...," he took a deep breath, "Mouth of yours and I'm arresting you for obstructing an investigation. Who out of you lot of wastrels has access?"

"All of us. The actors, make-up artists, set designers, producers, cameramen—"

"Okay. I've got it. How many?"

"Forty-three. We're a small, yet frightfully successful, company."

"Do all of them have a key?"

"Thirteen of us have unimpeded access."

"Jason, fetch some paper from the gift shop. I'm sure they can spare a notebook. Mr Lovelady, I'll need you to write down their names."

Notebook provided, Xavier did as he was asked. His voice a deep purr he said, "There you have it dear boy. All the information you need."

The trigger itch was back. "Not quite. How does everyone get on in your wee company?"

"Love each other to bits. We're one big happy family in Pink Play Productions."

Who the frick came up with that god-awful name? Things just get worse. Maybe a move to traffic wouldn't be quite so bad after all.

The questioning continued but pulling wisdom teeth with doll's tweezers would have been easier. It left Roy feeling he would like to dump Xavier, and every last person in Pink Play Productions, into the Tay. He was saved from career suicide by Nina's arrival. She was sporting a pair of Hunter wellies.

Abigail was long gone having lost the will for any of it.

"It's ninety degrees in the shade. What's with the wellies? You going paddling in the river?"

"Orders from on high. Shona didn't think much to the yellow high heels I was wearing."

"You don't say? What you doing here? Come for a cuppa in the cafe have you?"

"I've come to ask the Viking here some questions. Don't be so cheeky to your sergeant."

"I could kiss you, Sergeant. Here, have him with my compliments. I'll throw in a couple of Mars Bars for good measure."

"Deal." She turned to Xavier Lovelady whose brow was arranged in a puzzled frown. His brain, obviously a couple of lines short of a scene, was struggling to keep up. "Your crew's hanging about in the cafe. Please could you come with me? We need to know if they are all accounted for."

"Ship's crew or film crew?" The bluster had disappeared from his voice as he took in the enormity of the situation.

"Both." Nina's voice was soft. "Come on. I'll be right there with you."

He stood up, no longer a confident actor but an old man with the weight of the world on his shoulders. His world anyway.

5

A battering ram of sound flooding from the cafe slammed into them as they entered. It couldn't have been louder if they had assembled the entire cast of Ringling Brothers Circus. A tsunami of bodies surged towards Xavier when he entered. A bunch of strapping coppers held them at bay.

"Stay where you are. I'll no' be saying it again. We've cells available for anyone who feels they'd rather be somewhere other than this cafe."

The copper winked at Nina, who grinned at him.

"Good on you Archie. Keep them on the straight and narrow." She gripped Xavier's arm just as he was disappearing into the crowd. "You're staying right here with me."

His va va voom had returned with vigour. "I need—"

"To do exactly what I tell you. Does everyone in this gaggle belong to you?"

"Many of them are part of my company. The others I lay no claim to."

"Roy, split them up. Film crew versus anyone else," she yelled.

"What? Did you say put the film crew in cells?"

"Don't be such an eejit. Put everyone into two groups."

With some hustle, bustle, yelling, shuffling and a great deal of encouragement the bodies were sorted and arranged.

"Lovelady, anyone missing?" Nina had dragged him into the middle of the crowd that identified themselves with him. Nina could have worked it out without sorting them out. The luvvies all flying hands and animated gestures were yelling fit to bust about film time. The remainder stood arms crossed, with eyes throwing mutinous looks in the direction of the cops.

"Three look like they've failed to report. Not an unusual occurrence as we all spent the night at the Robert Falcon Scott public house."

"It's the Rabbie round these parts," said Roy.

"Dear boy, I could never call it that. It is a desecration of the name of one of the finest men to live."

Roy's features rearranged themselves into a look that said, call me dear boy again and you wont be able to speak for a month. Nina grabbed his arm before he could take one step.

"Later Roy," she muttered.

Roy's features rearranged themselves into a slight lift of one side of his mouth. For now, content to leave it. *Revenge a dish served cold and all that.*

"Names?"

He rattled them off.

"Roy, get them down. I'm off to chat to the glaring minority."

As she approached, muttering broke out amidst a general move towards her.

"Can't do..."

"Flaming cheek."

"Who do the police..."

One man detached himself from the rabble. From his suit, pink shirt and mickey mouse tie, Nina deduced he was the leader of the mob. Even at five foot eleven she had to crane her neck to look up at him.

"It's the middle of summer. I need to open up to the public."

The manager? "I need to ask you and your staff to

remain here. We'll have to speak to you."

"What's going on?"

"We can't say at the moment. Could you come with me?" Shona had approached.

"And who exactly are you to be ordering me around?"

Shona shoved her ID card in his face. "DI Shona McKenzie. This says I can do any amount of ordering I want. Now can we go to your office so I can talk to you quietly?"

The man turned on his heel, head held high, and strode off. Shona followed her long legs working hard to keep up. Not something Shona, the long-distance runner, was used to.

The manager, all bluster and outraged sensibilities, was called Giuseppe Jacobucci.

"Mr Jacobucci, I appreciate this causes all manner of problems for you but we are currently investigating a suspicious death."

"This is our busiest time of year. We must open. This is a disaster."

"As I say I appreciate your concern. However, the poor soul lying on the dock out there is having a worse day than you. They are *my* main concern."

The bluster and posturing continued for a couple of minutes. Shona kept quiet until vague normality returned.

"Mr Jacobucci which of your staff members has access to the film set?"

"None of them. They've got it locked down tighter than the Royal Bank's vaults."

"Are you telling me no one can get into the ship? Hard to believe."

"They can get access to the ship when there is no filming taking place onboard. We were meant to be opening today. That's why—"

"I heard you the first time Mr Jacobucci. You will not be opening today and I need to speak to all of your staff. Please make somewhere available so we can interview everyone."

"You can't commandeer my offices." His puffed out chest gave him the look of an angry, fat pigeon.

"You're absolutely right. I can't. I will need them all to come down to the station. That should add several hours onto the investigation and your ship's downtime."

The arrogant attitude was replaced with bustling helpfulness. A room, coffee and cakes were made available.

Sometimes I love this job.

6

Trudging along the corridor, a condemned-man look on his face, Xavier Lovelady put one weary foot in front of the other. He hesitated at the door as his foot refused to step over the threshold. The outside world was now a terrifying place.

"Xavier, I need you to do this." A comforting hand on his back nudged him gently forward. Shona had asked the director if he would mind taking a look. He might be able to identify the body.

The man somehow managed to lift his foot and place it down again. He was surprised to find his other foot followed suit. He swerved to avoid the historical props that lent authenticity to the Victorian era scenes. Stopping beside a mountainous heap of coal he said, "I can't do it. What if I know him?"

That's what I was hoping. "You're not on your own. I'll be with you."

A few more hesitant steps and he'd veered around the coal. He stumbled as his foot scuffed a rope. Caught his balance and then, realising what he was looking at, his face went white. He grabbed Shona's arm and clutched it. He staggered again.

"Xavier. Are you okay?"

Xavier's mouth opened. Closed. Opened again but no sound came out.

"Mr Lovelady?"

Shona's urgent voice pierced the fog that had entered his brain. "Yes." It was barely a whisper. He tried again, stronger this time. "Yes, I'm okay."

Shona's voice was gentler but kept its firmness. "Do you know him?"

"It's...it's..." He swallowed several times. "Martin. One of my company." His voice resumed its previous strength as he talked about his favourite subject. "He played the ship's cook."

"Does Martin have a surname?"

"Martin Crook-Statham. Truly brilliant actor. Much undervalued."

"What was his relationship like with the rest of the film crew?"

"Everyone loved him."

"I've not been around many film crews but I'm sure that's not true. I'm sure many gigantic egos got in the way of that being the case."

Xavier's arms were waving about like a conductor on speed. "How dare you? This company is tight-knit, supportive and—"

Shona took a step towards him and leaned in close. She kept a weather eye on the flailing arms. "A bunch of actors. All of whom probably wanted to be top dog. Let's not forget the supporting cast of characters, costume, make-up etc."

She turned away and shouted to Roy. "Get yourself over here."

Roy hurried to do her bidding. "'Sup?"

"Talk properly Roy. You're not fourteen. Help Mr Lovelady to round up his company. We'll need to interview every last bally one of them. Get them to report to Bell Street station."

Thinking fondly of Gulag Bell Street she nevertheless went to find the rest of the team. "How's the evidence hunt going. Anything turned up?"

"One sapphire earring found just under the camera dolly. Couple of cigarette ends nearby. A few empty sandwich wrappers and crisp bags. Saying that, apart from the modern day rubbish it would be difficult to tell wit's props and wit's evidence," delivered in Peter's usual tone of gloom and doom.

A groan escaped from Shona's lips. "I hadn't thought of that. What a pigging nightmare."

"That will need some skilful questioning to sort out."

"And you're the woman for it. Well volunteered Abigail."

"What? I didn't..." She gave in to the inevitable. "Can I keep someone with me?"

"Iain, you're on. Take photos as you go round. Jason, you can stay as well. Take notes. Wait until the body's gone before you return to HQ."

"Aye, aye captain." Jason gave a smart salute.

"Wrong salute soldier boy. This is the navy, no' the army."

"Trust you to know that."

"I know everything, laddie. Dinnae you forget it."

"Wouldn't dream of it."

Shona pulled her phone out of her handbag and rang Roy. She broke the news that anyone involved with props should stay. They would be assisting Abigail with her enquiries.

Stopping only to dump her handbag in her box-sized office, Shona went to update the Chief. Still stinging from her last bollocking for keeping things from him, she didn't want a repeat performance. Giving him the bare essentials she was finished in a few minutes.

The look in his eyes indicated he considered Shona to be a halfwit.

"Are you telling me my station is going to be packed full of actors?"

"Yes, Sir."

"Are you a blithering idiot? They'll be a right bunch of clowns. It'll take you a fortnight to get a sensible answer from any one of them."

That's a bit general. Peacekeeping won out over a smart answer. "Yes, Sir. We'll do our best to speed it up."

"Make sure you do, Inspector. I will not tolerate my station being used as a half-way house for a bunch of thespians."

She left, practising her usual sport of planning the Chief's demise. Swinging from a noose strung from the lamp post outside the main door of the station was the current favourite.

"So what did the Chief say then, Ma'am?" Peter laughed.

"He's delighted that we are on top of the situation and investigating thoroughly."

"Aye right. We're no' ordering cakes for the luvvies then?"

"Suffice to say we will conduct our interviews in a

timely manner. Get the remainder of the team together. We'll divvy up the interrogations."

"Interrogations? I like the cut of your jib. Ma'am."

Several hours later, Shona had a headache and the urge to kill every single actor or actress she ever encountered. She also had a large mug of coffee and the whole team in the briefing room.

"Is it an actor's job description that they need to lie through their teeth?"

"Their stories are more bent than they are," said Peter.

"You're right. As camp as a field full of tents," added Roy.

"Roy that's quite enough. How many warnings do you need about respect?"

"What? I was agreeing with Peter."

"You stupid little sod. I was talking about them being crooked, no' gay. Whit way they swing's up to them."

"I know. I wasn't saying anything."

"For heaven's sake pull it back together." She leaped to her feet and grabbed a board pen. She pulled the top off and carefully wrote down the name of the murder victim. It sat lonely and accusing in a sea of white, the harsh lights turning it green with a hint of bile.

"What do we know about him?"

The silence could have been used as wallpaper paste.

"Nina, give me something." Her eyes narrowed as she fixed them on her sergeant.

"Martin's not his real name. He's actually called Jedediah Ramsbottom."

"No wonder he ditched it. Imagine using that on a movie trailer," said Abigail. "Doesn't exactly make the girls swoon."

"Does Jedediah have a family?"

"His father's Louis Starkind." This was delivered with nonchalance and more than a hint of glee.

"The actor? You're telling me Jedediah is his son?"

"Yep. The one and only Louis Starkind, living legend and star of most movies for the past thirty years. The very one."

Chatter broke out. Shona, too involved in her own thoughts, didn't do anything to stop it. She couldn't form a sentence if she tried. *How could I not know this? The Chief will blow his stack. I might as well prepare my own noose now.*

"You couldn't have given me this nugget before now? What took you so long?"

"To be fair, I've only just found out"

"Has anyone broken the news to him that his son is now in our mortuary?"

"Probably half the film crew," said Peter. "I'm sure they love a bit of gossip."

"Roy, get me his number."

Whipping out his phone Roy tapped the screen a few times and obliged.

"I'm off to ring him. You lot, start filling that whiteboard in. See if you can make a few connections. Maybe you'll have solved it all by the time I reappear."

By some miracle known only to the gods of the universe, Jedediah's father did not know about his untimely demise. Louis Starkind's cultured tone informed Shona he was unimpressed. Unimpressed mind you, not broken-hearted or devastated. That told her a lot about the relationship between father and son. The cultured tone also informed her that his private jet and a limousine service would have him in her office in under three hours. No, he did not want them to pick him up from the airport. He wouldn't be seen dead in a flea ridden police car. All sorts of criminals and undesirables would have been resident inside said vehicle. That told her a lot about Louis Starkind's personality.

"Ignorant, jumped up egomaniac," she informed the team. "I'd rather have Auld Jock in the station than him."

Auld Jock, a station favourite, was a man of the road, or a tramp to use the popular term. They all loved him and his dog, Fagin. He spent a lot of time in the nick, not for nefarious reasons, but getting a feed for him and Fagin the Thief.

"What's he said that's wound you up, Ma'am?" Abigail was brave enough to say what the rest of them were thinking.

"Wound me up! Wound me up?" She stopped gritted her teeth and outlined his argument in full, with added embellishments in the way of hand movements. "When he gets here I might just nick the noose from evidence. He'll be swinging from it."

With twitching lips the others managed to keep their laughter swallowed down.

Nina, the fashionista, on the other hand, "I wouldn't do that. Prison clothes are not a good look." She shuddered for good effect. This led to an explosion of laughter and much spraying of coffee over various documents.

"Could you make any more mess? Get this cleaned up." Shona tried the grim look but it turned into laughter.

"Get a grip. We've a murder to solve."

"Won't be long before it's murders plural, Ma'am. Not with you involved." Roy practised his usual sport of living life on the edge.

Shona's look said he was close to joining the Chief and Louis in the queue for the noose.

By the time she had an update on everyone from the film crew Shona had a headache that would only be calmed by several gallons of industrial-strength coffee. Talk about convoluted. After several hours they'd managed to figure out the main players in their current drama. These were on the whiteboard and plain for all to see:

Felix Fotheringham- Farington, best friend of the deceased and playing the part of Captain Scott.

Xavier Lovelady, director of the movie.

Darren Spottiswood, playing the part of Scott's right hand man.

Sonya Chey, an American actress playing the part of Scott's wife, Kathleen.

Sarah Martrand, Martin's girlfriend and groupie to the stars.

Della Fantine, make-up artist.

Stephen Dolman, Martin's understudy.

Francesco Esposito, wardrobe assistant who spent several nights in the pub with Martin.

Hui Chao, a Buddhist monk and spiritual advisor to several of the crew.

Zander Young playing the part of Ernest Shackleton.

"Let's unravel things a bit further. What do we know about them all?"

"Virtually nothing. They're all playing the 'He was a wonderful man' card," said Nina.

"Yeah, right. And the penguin statues in town have all come to life. What I wouldn't give for a witness who spills the beans about everything right away."

"That would be too easy, Ma'am. You wouldn't like

it if you didn't have a puzzle to solve," said Iain.

"There're puzzles and there're puzzles. A three hundred piece, instead of a ten thousand piece would be nice." She tapped the whiteboard with the pen. "Concentrate. This board's too empty. Let's solve this murder."

Shona tapped the name of Hui Chao. "What makes him worthy of our interest?"

"Me and Peter did that one. They had a number of meetings over the last several weeks. He wanted to know more about the Buddhist religion."

"I'm no' so sure about his intentions, there. He spent his life in the pub. Couldnae have been that serious about being a Buddhist. Maybe the monk took the hump and decided to do away with him."

"It's as good a theory as any. Not top of my list though."

The remainder of the team clattered through the door, chattering loudly and carrying huge mugs of coffee. They'd returned from interviewing the staff at Discovery Point.

"Welcome back. We'll get your report in a minute. Sit down and listen."

"Isn't Buddhism meant to be a peaceful religion? Doesn't go well with murder" Nina continued their previous conversation. "Bit like Sikhism on that score."

"That'd be a perfect disguise for a serial killer. No one would ever guess," said Jason. "Just think how long you could get away with bumping people off. Brilliant."

"Seriously. You're speculating on how good it would be to get away with murder?"

"Hey, Soldier Boy. That's not nice."

"Shut up, Roy. You're just as bad. You'd have said it if you'd thought about it. You brace of idiots should grow up." With great effort and steely determination, she managed to stop herself from smiling. *This pair will be the death of me.*

The information was added to their outline. "Worth exploration. See if there's anything on our monk out there in cyberspace. Roy, your task."

"With pleasure." He rubbed his hands together and leapt from his chair.

"Sit down, Superman. Leave the tights and underpants aside for the minute. There might be more for you."

He landed with a thump in his chair and slumped down. "Aww. I was looking forward to dishing the dirt."

"Roy, for heaven's sake, the poor man is probably a model of decorum. Keep an open mind."

"Felix Fotheringham-Farington. I'll pick him up," said Shona, "Best buddy of the deceased since they started at boarding school together when they were four."

"He's a top actor, Ma'am. How did they get him for a two-bit movie set in Dundee?" Shona nodded. Felix had won many an Oscar and here he was in Pink Play Productions. *Sounds like a porno outfit. Could they have chosen a worse name?*

"Even I've heard o' him," said Peter. "And Dundee may be bonnie and all that, but it's no' exactly Hollywood."

"That's something we'll need to pick up. I want to ask him a few more questions. Iain, find out if he's still here and ask him to hang around."

"He got Martin his part. Seems like our corpse wasn't doing so well with the acting." Nina stood up and demonstrated her own acting abilities. Striking a pose, she looked so like Felix, it was uncanny. "The poor boy just could not get a break and yet he was a truly brilliant actor. Stunning in his brilliance in fact. One has to question the intellect of many producers, I feel."

"Blimey, Nina, you're good." Roy's eyes weren't just saucers, they were plates. "You're in the wrong career."

"Nah, I'd much rather be chasing criminals through mud. Much more fun than the glamorous life of an actor."

"He sounds like a right ponce," said Abigail.

"I wouldn't let his wife hear you say that. She's some sort of minor European princess. A princess no less," said Shona.

"Jeez, Hollywood royalty and real royalty all wrapped up in one murder case," said Roy. "Some case this. Even weirder than our normal offering."

"Yep. Eggshells and walking will be our watchwords. We will not give the Chief anything to complain about."

"Ma'am, I dinnae mean to be difficult but it's way past home time. I've to go and see the young lass in her school concert. Any chance we could pick all this up in the morning?"

"And I've a murder to investigate. Still, you're right. Off home with the lot of you. I've a cat to feed anyway."

"Cat? Not on your life. You're off for a night on the town with the Procurator Fiscal."

Shona rolled up the whiteboard cloth and lobbed it at Nina. "Cheeky git. Shut up and get home or I'll have you on file duty for the night."

Nina, as always wasn't phased by the treat. She laughed and threw the cloth back.

Most of the team weren't there to hear this threat. Nina grabbed her jacket and fled. Switching off the lights Shona headed home via the Chief's office. She wanted to update him on the royal princess situation. Taking a deep breath and squaring her shoulders she pushed open the door to his office.

8

Shona woke up bright and early and went for a run along the seafront. Overnight thunderstorms had abated leaving the sky iridescent blue with clouds which made the word fluffy seem inadequate. The sun hadn't yet turned up the dial on the temperature so it was perfect for maintaining a brisk pace. Her model-length legs made easy work of the distance involved as she ran towards Monifieth. A hint of a breeze played around her, caressing her with a gentle touch. It was almost perfect. The one imperfection was high overhead. She could hear the raucous caw of gulls as they pirouetted overhead. One swooped down, the caaw growing more harsh. Shona ducked a microsecond before its claws became entangled in her blond ponytail. Frantically waving her hands she sent the gull with attitude on its merry way. Or so she hoped.

The gull reminded her of the Chief the previous evening. He'd been stepping out the door to go home when she caught him. Both her information and his delay in getting back to Mrs Chief Inspector sent him into orbit. The general gist of his displeasure was her ability to attract chaos whenever she undertook an investigation. Could she not do this calmly and without attracting attention from every notable person in a two thousand mile radius? His final parting shot was, "If you come in here and tell me the President of the USA is involved, your employment will be terminated."

Shona left with the feeling she'd like to terminate him. Permanently. With a gun.

She passed someone talking on a mobile, loudly, whilst gesticulating like a conductor in the wilder bits of the 1812 Overture. Man? Woman? Transvestite? It was hard to tell. Shona's investigative instincts kicked up a couple of gears. The slim build of a woman, with female hair, yet the rugged face of a man and a deep gravelly voice. Maybe a woman who had smoked sixty a day since the age of nine? Maybe a man embracing his feminine side? Such deep thoughts took her another couple of miles into her run and helped her pick up her pace.

By the time she returned to her flat for a shower, Shakespeare had just about forgiven last night's tardiness in providing her dinner. Shakespeare, a wee lassie cat, had refused any change of name so Shakespeare she remained. By the time Shona had delivered some gourmet salmon concoction into her bowl the forgiveness was complete. She rubbed herself against Shona's legs, purring and meowing as she headed towards the bowl. *If only all life's problems were solved with a dish of salmon dinner.*

As she drove to work in her brand new Melbourne Red BMW Shona had a feeling that something was not quite right. A sensation of impending doom hung over her head ready to descend at the slightest thought. When she realised it was because she hadn't been called in early to a dead body she cheered out loud. Cranking up the volume on the top of the range stereo she belted out the Kaiser Chiefs in time to the song coming from the speakers. Life couldn't be better. The sun was promising another heatwave and she only had one murder to solve not half a dozen. Add to that she was wearing a new summer frock that complemented her colour perfectly, and all was well in her world.

Her mood crashed as she walked through the portals of Gulag Bell Street. Her thoughts had convinced her she'd be met by news of a murder.

Instead, as she arrived at the team's office, she was met by an egg roll and a cup of coffee.

"Get this doon you, Ma'am. It'll give you strength for the interviews."

Peter wasn't known for his generosity so Shona grabbed the roll whilst she could and swallowed it down. The coffee was hot, freshly brewed and rich.

"What's going on? Are you trying to sweeten me up for something?"

"No' at all, Shona. My bus got me here early so I thought we could start the day fortified."

A lightbulb flashed in Shona's brain. "Has the wife got you sticking to that diet again?"

He had the grace to look a bit sheepish. "Aye. The eggs were boiled though, no' fried so I'm okay. Doreen and Annie made a lovely fresh batch for us."

Shona determined that she would use this as ammunition to blackmail him for months. The only person Peter was afraid of was his wife.

The briefing room smelt of cold coffee and stale sandwiches. This had a lot to do with the fact that both were liberally scattered around the room.

"Where's Mo? She's usually got the place spick and span for us."

"Her husband's had a stroke. She's up the hospital," said Abigail "Not looking good so she said."

"Down to us then. Take all this crap to the kitchen. We'll wash up later. Remind me to get Mo a card as well."

A couple of hours later and they were going round in circles trying to work out the convoluted relationships amongst the members of the film crew. They'd pretty much ruled out the staff at Discovery Point. They were all longstanding and had no grudge against the film crew. In fact they fascinated them.

Abigail filled them in. "The young women are all in love with every last actor especially the male ones. Apart from Titania Fairbairn who's in love with Sonya Chey. As are a couple of the younger men."

"So you're telling me that everything's on the straight and narrow?"

"Giuseppe didn't want the filming to take place. Complained vociferously to everyone including his local MP. Changed his mind pronto the minute the got the smell of money. A huge fat cheque shut him up."

"How much money are we talking about?"

Abigail paused. She waited until Shona leaned forward with her mouth open to speak before saying, "More dosh than we'll ever see. One point four million quid to be exact."

Slack-jawed, Roy said, "You what? For a tinpot film?"

"I wouldn't use the term tinpot but I agree it does seem an extraordinary amount."

"They might need to hand it back if the filming doesn't go to schedule," said Nina. "They've strict contracts for these movies."

"For a copper you seem to know a lot of weird sh—"

"Jason! You know the rules." Shona's glare could crack teeth at a trillion paces.

"Sorry, Ma'am."

"Get hold of the contract and check it out. Abigail, you and Jason can go when we've finished here."

This was not to be. As they were wrapping up the door opened and the duty sergeant walked in.

"Ma'am you and the team are needed urgently in Backmuir Woods. Seems they have a dead body requiring your attention."

"See, I knew there would be another dead body before too long," said Roy. "That'll be another serial killer for us then?"

"Stop speculating. It could be anything. Grab anything you need. I'll see you at Backmuir."

There was a stampede for the door. Shona could have sworn Jason was rubbing his hands. She definitely saw him and Roy doing a high five. *How can they be so excited about murder? Seriously, that's deranged.*

9

Mushrooms and murder. Not words you hear in the same sentence very often. But these were the very words Shona heard, or thought she heard. She bent closer to the elderly witness in the hope she could make sense of his incoherent ramblings. He was sitting on a tree stump on the edge of the forest. Several trees torn from their anchors, their roots dark crows' fingers against the bright blue sky, formed a macabre backdrop. It took a few minutes for Shona to work out what he was saying. It turned out he'd been out picking wild mushrooms when he fell over a dead body. Literally fell over it. The stains on his worn Harris Tweed jacket indicated this particular body was in an advanced state of decay. He looked a little decayed himself. A shrivelled gnome of a man he took the cliché of what an old man should look like to its furthest point. Then doubled it. A shaking and teeth-chattering wreck, it appeared he might be feeding the wild mushrooms with his own body soon.

"Abigail, could you take Mr Smith to the cafè in the village and get him a cup of tea?"

Abigail gently took the man's arm and helped him up. "I'll get a doctor to him as well. He'd better be checked out," she said in a low voice.

"Good thinking. Take a statement as well. Without helping him off to his grave that is."

Shona watched them go, and then headed towards the corpse. Deep inside a thick canopy of Scottish pine it nestled up against the bottom of a majestic tree. The pine acted as a sentinel for the grizzly find. Despite the bright day the darkness was thick this far into the

41

woods. The sun struggled to penetrate the thick canopy of leaves. Shona shivered in the cool air. The area, both physically and spiritually, was a direct contrast to the warmth on the edge of the woods. Evil mocked her and touched every surface with its icy tendrils.

The forest was classified as ancient and so was the corpse. Well, maybe not quite ancient, but definitely not fresh. As she approached the body she grabbed her nose over the paper mask she was wearing. She was beginning to regret the two bacon rolls she'd had for breakfast. They were threatening to rejoin society and the rotting body on the ground. She pulled a mint from her pocket, hurriedly unwrapped it, pulled the mask away from her face, and stuffed the sweet in her mouth. Sucking hard she approached the body.

If this body was linked to their existing case then their killer had been at it for a number of years. *Possible but not probable,* thought Shona. *Still, keep an open mind.* More skeleton than body, the top half protruded from the soil like a rotting stump. Shona was left wondering how the man could have managed to trip over it. She might suggest he visit an optician. Squatting down she peered at the area. Few insects. She looked around. Little vegetation. From her limited knowledge of all things forensic she knew that meant the body was in an advanced state of decay. She was willing to leave the rest of the forensic work to Mary.

"What's unearthed it at this late stage?"

"Knowing you, Ma'am, probably the bear from Camperdown Park," said Peter.

"Ha flaming ha. Everyone's a comedian."

"How the heck do I know? Could be anything," said Jason.

"Don't be so cheeky, Jason. That was bordering on insolence."

"Looks like it's foxes. I've been photographing the

ground. There're fox tracks everywhere."

"Ooh, our very own Bear Grylls," said Nina. "Last night's torrents on top of the winter's downpours could have loosened most of the topsoil. That leaves room for Brer Fox and his mates to tuck in for a tasty meal."

"Nina. More respect. Whoever this poor individual is they deserve that at least."

"Sorry, Ma'am. I didn't mean it the way it came out."

"I should jolly well hope not. I'm disappointed in you. You're a sergeant and should be setting an example."

Nina's slumped shoulders indicated she truly was sorry. An unusual occurrence as her fallback position was usually laughter.

Shona took in her sergeant's demeanour and said, "Let's leave it there. We've a murder to investigate."

They turned back to the body. "Not too close. Spread out and get a search going." She grabbed Roy's arm and yanked him back from the edge of the area. "Easy, Tiger. I'll get up close and personal with this bit. Or rather Mary will when she gets here."

"The Procurator Fiscal's no' here, Ma'am. Are you sure he's okay?"

"I'm sure he's busy doing whatever PFs do. Heavens, man. He doesn't have to come to every crime scene."

"No' even if you're at it?"

"Especially if I'm at it. Go organise that lot in a search and stop persecuting me." She gestured towards a gap in the trees where the team had congregated.

Peter's booming laugh rang out as he left. A red squirrel darted down a tree and bolted past the body.

"Peter, I swear—"

"Aye, I know. Traffic."

I need a new threat. Note to self. Think of

something suitable.

Mary, all four foot eleven of her, was as cheery and helpful as ever when she turned up.

"Back of beyond, just what I expected of you Shona."

"You'd think the references to me being a serial killer would have worn off by now."

"Not a chance. My whole department keep themselves entertained thinking of new ones. We might need to move onto the colonies next. We're running out of the British version."

"I keep you lot in business so I don't know what you're moaning about?"

"More business than we ever want or need."

This pleasant exchange was accompanied by Mary examining the area. Despite her humour her keen professionalism was apparent.

"Has Iain got all the photographs he needs so far?"

"Yep. Do you need him back?"

"Please. I'd like him to get certain angles for me."

Shona trotted off at a rapid clip and returned with Iain of the supersize lens. Mary gave him instructions. Iain did as he was told. Mary and her team got up close and personal with the corpse. Iain took more photos. Shona leaned against a nearby tree and kept a weather eye on proceedings.

"Anything I can do to help?"

"Not so far. I'll give you a yell if you've something else to do."

"I'll go and join the search. Not that I'm thinking anything will be thrown up after all this time."

Mary wasn't paying a blind bit of notice. She was engrossed in taking samples and carefully removing dirt from around the body. It was a joy to see her professionalism and respect for the body in her care.

Peter had whipped the troops into order. They were forming an efficient fan and looking at the surroundings with great detail. Whilst this was an area of natural beauty, not many walkers penetrated this far. Trees and vegetation grew together in a dense tangle making it demanding for easy access. Most of the local population kept to the edges of the woods where there were pleasant walks and pathways. A crash and a yell made Shona jump.

"What's happened?" She set off in the direction of the shout. Undergrowth pulled at her feet, slowing her down.

"Jason, the walking disaster, has just head-butted a tree," shouted Nina.

Shona stopped short beside him. "Are you hurt?"

He was rubbing his head where an ostrich sized bump was materialising in front of their eyes. "That hurt like a bast..."

"Shut it Jason. Nina, take him to find Abigail. She'll have paramedics with her for our witness."

As they left she yelled, "Come straight back, Nina."

Experience told her she'd lose them for the best part of an hour. One of the paramedics was Nina's latest squeeze. Given that Shona was usually chatting to her boyfriend over a dead body she couldn't take her sergeant to task. Plus, the paramedic was quite dishy and the sort of chap you'd like to spend time with.

The search continued with little result. A torn piece of cloth from a low-slung tree branch was bagged and tagged. A discarded tissue and a random crisp packet followed this into more bags.

"More than likely the crisp packet and the tissues blew in on the wind. The cloth might be a bit more meaningful."

"There's a footprint in a patch of damp earth. I've got some cracking photos and a nice little cast."

"Iain, you're a positive wunderkind." Shona's eyes shone with admiration. "What would we do without you?"

"The place would go straight to hell, Ma'am."

"It probably would to be honest. You lot get back to the station. I'll get an update from Mary and join you there."

10

Shona didn't get as far as her car before a strikingly beautiful black woman wearing a canary yellow dress and orange shoes accosted her. Adanna Okifor was a local reporter with whom Shona had a love/hate relationship. That meant Adanna loved getting information from Shona. Shona hated the fact she had to have anything to do with the woman, or anything to do with the press in general. She'd grudgingly formed an uneasy truce with the reporter.

"What do you want?"

"That's not a nice way to speak to me." Adanna took a couple of steps to the side and went to move round Shona.

Shona performed a quick shimmy blocking her way. "Stay right there. I don't have time for niceties. I take it you're after info?"

"As much as you can give me."

"That'll be none then."

"I heard there was a dead body in the woods."

"I don't know where from. Did you bury it there or something?"

"So there is a dead body? Is it a murder?"

"I didn't say that and I refuse to speculate. Buzz off."

"Give me something."

"I will. Back at the station with the rest of the press."

"Come on Shona, play nicely. I'm always helping you when I can."

"Very civil of you I'm sure." She relented. "Yes, there's a dead body. That's all you're getting from me.

You'll get more with the rest of them."

"A quick photo?" Adanna's grin indicated she knew she was chancing her mitt.

"Do you think I came down in last night's thunderstorm? I'll walk you back to your car. I'm going that way anyway."

They parted company as Shona waved Adanna off in her canary yellow convertible. Shona climbed in her car and pointed the nose in the direction of Bell Street. She knew it wouldn't be long before the woman appeared in her office. It would appear that Adanna might be a direct descendent of a Mountie. She always got her man or, in this case, her story. She'd certainly managed to sway Shona over to thinking she was moderately palatable. No mean feat given Shona's pathological hatred of the press.

11

As she walked through the doors of the station there were three people and a dog taking up residence in the waiting room. One young lad with ripped jeans and a denim jacket stuffed in his rucksack was fast asleep, head lolling. Earphones in and an intellectual paperback slack in his hands he appeared to be a student. A young Chinese woman, sheaf of papers in hand, was muttering to herself as her finger moved across the paper. She paused and pushed black glasses up her nose. She paid Shona no heed. Shona wondered if they were using the nick as a quiet study area. The third occupant was Auld Jock, whom Shona was delighted to see. The dog was Fagin, a Weimaraner, and their resident thief. He could smell a treat at a million paces and knew Shona had a cake about her person. He currently had her pinned against a wall as he rummaged in her bag.

"Fagin, come here."

The dog, for once, did as he was told. However, he was clutching his spoils of war. The cake fell to the ground and Fagin proceeded to wolf it down in three seconds flat.

"Jock, you've really got to train him. Cake's not good for him."

"I've used every trick in the book, lassie. Thon dog whisperer would struggle with this one."

Shona, having looked after Fagin when he was a puppy, just shook her head. The dog was a joy to look at, friendly, and hell on four oversized paws.

"What brings you to the Bell Street Hilton?"

"Fagin wanted to see you."

"Did he also want to see a couple of sausages?"

"Aye, he did, Shona."

"Follow me to the canteen. I'm sure Annie will feed the pair of you like the royalty you are."

"Och, away with you Shona." Despite the remonstration the grin was splitting his face. The Chief was out by the time Shona had finished sorting out Jock. According to his secretary he'd be out for the remainder of the day. He'd gone to a meeting with the Chief Constable. That was code for they'd gone for lunch and a game of golf. Then she felt guilty as the Chief Constable, a top man, wouldn't get up to such shenanigans. The Chief on the other hand? She scribbled down a message about the latest case and booked in a press release for the next morning at 9 am. This got her off the hook and delayed the inevitable bollocking.

There wasn't a lot she could do about the *Mystery of the Corpse in the Wood*. Mary had to finish and release the area to them properly. Her findings might help them discover the identity. This would give her something to hold on to. The evidence from the scene was on its way to the lab and might give them some clue as to a possible direction. A cup of coffee and an update of HOLMES was calling. The Home Office Large or Major Enquiry System was amazing and had made things a lot easier for coppers in the UK. However, if he wasn't regularly fed he spat his dummy out. Typical man. If the computer had been named MARPLE it would have been much more easy to appease. This thought had her laughing to herself, a mad woman in full flow.

"So, just exactly where have you all been? I've been back almost half an hour."

"Sorry, Ma'am. We went and grabbed a spot of lunch on the way back." Peter handed over a paper bag.

"We've a brace of murders on our hands and you think it's fine and dandy to stop for snacks. Get a grip and get yourself along to the briefing room."

As the others scurried off she glanced in the bag. She resisted the temptation to wolf down a sausage roll and threw the bag on the top in the kitchen. She did stop long enough to write her name on it. There were more thieves inside the station than outside. Any sausage roll found loafing would be appropriated by anyone feeling the gnawing pangs of hunger. This one had her name on it, literally.

"Apart from your stomachs has anyone had any thoughts re our cases?"

"With the *Hanging in the Harbour* I think we need to untangle the convoluted relationships between the film crew."

"I agree. I'm sure that lot have got more twists than a hangman's noose."

"If you don't mind me sayin', Ma'am, you're a right pair of jokers."

Shona glanced at Peter, bit back a retort, and turned her attention back to the full room.

"Roy, hot foot it and do a search. See what you can come up with on our monk."

"Awesome." He disappeared from view not once looking back. Roy and the dark web seemed to be bosom buddies. Shona wasn't quite sure how he'd gained these skills. They came in so useful she was willing to let it pass. To a point. There was only so much she could do to keep the Chief at bay. After that the boy was on his own.

"Abigail, did you manage to get a statement from mushroom man?"

"I did. He was a wee bit confused though. I think he was in shock. Might be worth interviewing him again. I only got halfway there as the paramedics carted him off in the direction of A&E."

"You can go up to Ninewells Hospital when we've finished. See if they've admitted him and get a statement if he's in a fit state.

Jason, pin down that contract. See if the money reverts if there are any delays.

Iain, you're on photos. I need them uploaded and in glorious, sharp, technicolour. I need the make of shoe from the cast."

The pair trooped from the room leaving Nina and Peter. "You pair are on interview duty with me. Get the collected cast back again. Let's tie them up in so many knots they'll think they're a lanyard."

She walked along to the interview room brushing pastry crumbs from her mouth. The thespians had surprised her by tipping up within the hour. Technical difficulties had stopped filming so they were free and baying for blood. Xavier stormed into the station spitting and bellowing like a camel in full rut. His willing acolytes trailed behind generating their own brand of clamour. Shona swallowed down a couple of preventative paracetamol along with her sausage roll. She had a feeling it was going to be a long day.

"Shut up!" She'd walked into the interview room straight into a battering ram of sound. Her order had no effect. She hollered it again, 30 decibels louder and with an added desk bang just to prove her point. Xavier stopped mid-flow. He stood up and opened his mouth.

"Sit down and keep your mouth shut. You will keep a civil tongue in your head in my nick. Got it?"

"How da—"

"I dare. One more word out of that gob of yours, unless I ask you a question, and I'll lock you up for disturbing the peace."

Xavier folded his arms and leaned back in his chair, with a face like a depressed pit bull, but at least he was quiet.

Big baby. Goes off in a huff cause a lassie's shouted at him.

"I don't believe all the guff about you lot being one big happy family. Give me the real story."

Xavier set his face even more sternly and glared at her.

"Mr Lovelady. I don't have time for this. One of your actors is dead. Doesn't that concern you?"

He shot forward so quickly Shona moved back, startled.

"Of course it bothers me you stupid woman. How can I carry on with filming with one of my actors missing?"

"Call me that again and I'll gladly do time to knock you into the middle of next week. I've a dead body literally swinging from a rope. Now does anyone in your cast have a grudge against Jedediah?"

"No."

"If I find out you've been lying..." She clenched her teeth together and exhaled slowly through her nose. *I am never going to see another movie as long as I live.*

Abruptly changing tack she said, "Has Jedediah got an understudy? What's his name?"

Before he could answer there was a knock at the door. The desk sergeant walked over to Shona, bent down and whispered, "Louis Starkind is here."

Unfortunately, the desk sergeant's hearing was a bit iffy so his whisper was more of a shout. This set Xavier off.

"Louis? Dear Louis is here? I must see him." He

stood up and took one step towards the door.

"Sit down. I haven't finished with you." She turned to the Sergeant. "Put Mr Starkind in a waiting room. Offer him a coffee. I'll be with him as soon as I can."

"My dear girl, one does not keep Louis Starkind waiting."

"I've had just about enough of you. You will address me as Inspector and nothing else. Do I make myself clear? You will also answer all my questions, promptly and in full."

"There's no need to take that tone. I'll comply."

"Now, who was he at odds with? Don't give me any rubbish about everything being peace and love." The words peace and love were emphasised with curled fingers.

"In any group there has to be disagreements." *Time for a change of tack.*

She looked around, leaned towards the witness and spoke in a lowered tone. "Heck, we don't even like each other around here. Sometimes I'd like to strangle my sergeant." She glanced towards Nina, whose face was an enigmatic mask.

He laughed and Shona joined in. *Bingo.*

"You're right, Inspector. You've ferreted it out of me."

Supercilious git. Wonder if I'd get away with swinging him from a rope?

"Dish the dirt then."

"Darren Spottiswood and Martin had a little contretemps yesterday. Ended in fisticuffs."

"Two of your actors, one of whom is now dead, had a fistfight and you're only just telling me?"

"Dea..." He took in Shona's narrowed eyes. "Inspector, it was all over in minutes. Best of pals now. At least they were until Martin's unfortunate demise."

Unfortunate demise? That's a new one for murder.

I'd say swinging from a rope on a film set was more than unfortunate.

"What was your relationship like with Martin?"

He opened his mouth but Shona intervened. "If you say perfect I swear to God I will not be responsible for my actions. Not a court in the land would convict me."

"You're frightfully tense. I can recommend a good Buddhist monk who could help you with that. Good listener and all that."

"Answer the damn question."

"We had our ups and downs as anyone does. Nothing that would lead to my committing the unpardonable sin of murder."

"In that case what were these ups and downs?"

"I want a lawyer."

"Fine, but get a local one. If you tell me your lawyer is coming from London you can wait for him in a cell."

She took a deep breath. Interview terminated at 15.00 at the request of Mr Lovelady that he have his lawyer present."

She switched off the recording equipment. "Nina, help Mr Lovelady to find a lawyer."

Returning to her office she banged into Peter.

"Get me the strongest painkiller in this nick. Steal them from evidence if you have to."

"Your day's no' going well then?"

"If I see another actor this side of heaven it will be too soon. How are your interviews going?"

"It's all one big love party."

"You must have dragged something out of them."

"I was tempted to use my grandfather's truncheon."

"Can I borrow it?"

"With pleasure. I did get a couple of wee tidbits."

"Hallelujah. I thought we'd be tripping down the

love party road forever."

"Aye." Peter brought her up to speed with a few well chosen sentences.

"You're a star. I could kiss you but I think Mrs Johnston would kill me."

"The way she's feeling at the moment she'd probably hand me over."

"Oh dear. Fancy coming to interview Louis Starkind with me?"

"Lead the way, dear lady."

"Peter, I swear..." The rest of her sentence was drowned in Peter's booming laugh. Shona shook her head and moved in the direction of Interview Room 1. "Would you like to fetch Louis?" she threw over her shoulder.

In the interests of keeping the world famous star sweet she asked for coffee to be brought to the interview room. "In china mugs, not the usual chipped affairs." She was speaking to a bereaved father after all, not her number one suspect.

12

Louis, sitting proud in his chair, was tall with black hair and a long pointed nose. He had adopted an Indian outfit of tight churidar pants and a long achkan jacket, in the traditional mourning colour of white. Mourning colour for Hindus that is. Shona thought it was a bit odd but maybe he'd converted. *There again maybe he's just a luvvy.*

"Where did you get this swill from? I'm used to the finer things in life."

Shona, who'd given orders to grind fresh beans and use her own coffee maker, was unimpressed.

"This is a police station, Mr Starkind, not the Ritz. I am sorry for your loss."

"So sorry that you kept me waiting?"

"Unavoidable I'm afraid. I was doing my utmost to solve your son's murder."

"What exactly were you doing?"

"We are currently undertaking interviews to try and get a picture of what happened."

"My eldest son has died. That's what's happened. You sitting around talking isn't going to change that."

"I appreciate that Mr Starkind, but my sitting around talking will help us find out what happened to him, and convict a murderer."

"I demand justice. You will bring the full force of the law to this case. I insist you use all available manpower to find the person who carried out this heinous crime."

"What movie did that come from Mr Starkind." Shona's kept her tone light but the steel in her voice was apparent.

"What? What? How dare–"

"It was from 'The Darkest Hour'," said Peter. "The one where you're a lawyer acting on behalf of that elderly couple. Their daughter wi' Down's Syndrome was beaten to death."

Both Shona and Louis adopted astonished looks.

Peter's face had a flushed look. Pulling at his collar he said, "My lassie loves that movie. She's watched it about three hundred times."

"It may help us if there were more honesty and less acting, Mr Starkind. I appreciate you are upset but we do need to solve your son's murder. We can only do this if we believe the answers you give us."

"I wish to speak to your immediate superior."

"I'm afraid that's not possible at the moment. However, the minute he returns I shall let the Chief Inspector know you are here. I would like to ask you a few questions in the meantime."

Louis crossed one long leg over the other and embraced a languid pose. "Fire away. If it helps solve your crime I will answer any questions you wish to ask."

Solve my crime. Not his son's murder. Weird reaction from a grieving father. Shona caught Peter's eye. He raised a disbelieving eyebrow. She nodded slightly. All was not well between father and son. She could almost smell it. It was stronger than the overpowering eau de cologne that Starkind was wearing. *What kind of man, faced with his son's death, stops to drown himself in perfume? I suppose, though, that with his lifestyle the public persona is so ingrained it tops everything else.*

"Do you know if anyone had a grudge against Jedediah? Anyone who might want to do him harm?"

"Please, do not use the stupid name his useless mother gave him. It was me who made him change his name to Martin. No son of mine was going to be known by a ponced up biblical name."

"Are you a Hindu?"

"No. What gave you that idiotic notion?"

Despite wanting to strike out Shona kept her tone mild. "Your clothes would seem to indicate this."

"I spent time in India and often adopt their clothing style. It is comfortable, stylish and my public expect me to be different."

"I would think your son would expect your respect. Did he have any enemies?"

"How would I know? We led our own lives. Do you live your life in your father's pocket?"

Shona counted to ten. In Swedish. The only words she knew in the language it slowed her down and stopped her strangling most of her witnesses. "We may not see each other every day but my father would be able to answer that question. Are you telling me you knew nothing about your son?"

"I got his mother pregnant, paid for his upkeep and spent time with him during the holidays. I did my fatherly duties."

"So you've no clue what he was up to last night then?"

"Not a clue, Inspector. You might want to ask Felix Fotheringham-Farington. He seemed to worship the ground Martin walked on. A bit too close if you ask me."

"Thank you for your time, Mr Starkind. My sergeant will find you somewhere comfortable to wait for the Chief Inspector to return from his meeting."

13

Shona dropped into the Chief's secretary's office to break the news he was needed back at the station. She agreed to chivvy him along and to make sure he returned before knocking off for the night. Shona wondered if she could knock off before he returned. She decided against it as it would come back to haunt her the next day.

"So, Peter, what were these glorious revelations of yours?"

"Stephen Dolman, Martin's understudy, is in love with Martin's girlfriend. Now that Martin's out o' the picture the field's clear on all fronts for our Stephen."

"Would seem he's got several motives, but isn't it a bit obvious?"

"Could be calling our bluff."

"Could be. Let's interview the man. You can take the lead on it. Grab one of the others. They should be back soon."

She decided her headache might be down to caffeine withdrawal so put the remainder of the coffee to good use. Thus fortified she was ready to face Darren Spottiswood. Unfortunately, he'd already lawyered up so Shona was stuck with Margaret McClusky, the battleship in full sail with a bosom you could do the ironing on. She and her brother were the bane of Shona's existence. Shona wasn't particularly fond of lawyers as she thought they just cluttered the place up. On the whole she tolerated them as a necessary evil. This pair took her feelings to new heights. "Please God, spare me." She kept her voice low.

Nina heard her. "You taking up religion?"

"I'm gonna take up murder. With McCluskey and Runcie as my first victims."

"Naebody would blame you, Ma'am. Especially all the Scottish judges. They hate them as well."

"I reckon you'd get away with it, Shona."

"That's as maybe but we've a murder to solve. Come on. Gird your loins as we go face the battleship."

The battleship was in fine fettle. Shona hadn't even sat down before McCluskey laid into her. "Why have you arrested my client?"

"Arrested him? Where did you get that? I only want to ask him a few questions about his mate who's lying in the morgue."

"My client did not commit that murder."

"No one's saying he did. Stop being so dramatic. For heaven's sake stop talking. We'll never get home if I can't ask him some questions."

Amidst huffing, puffing and a billowing chest Margaret did as she was told.

The preliminaries over and the *video* on, Shona started. "Mr Spottiswood, what was your relationship with the deceased?"

Spottiswood looked like a pugilist who'd not come off well in any fight never mind his last one. Squat, with solid muscle, his eyes were close together above a nose that deviated to the right' and with a tilt upwards. This gave his rough voice a nasal twang. His unkempt hair, slightly too long, also fell over his eyes. Shona was puzzled as to how he could understudy for Martin. Surely they would need to look like each other. The only thing that was remotely the same about this pair was that they both had ginger hair. *What sort of operation is this?*

"What are you getting at? You saying we were gay? I'm not like that."

McCluskey opened her mouth. Shona cut her off at the pass. "No one is suggesting any such thing. Were you friends, colleagues, despised each other?"

"It was fine. We mainly just ignored each other."

"So were you just ignoring each other when you decided to punch the lights out of each other yesterday?"

"Who told you that, love? Load of lies."

Shona glanced at his knuckles which were bruised and swollen. "Your hands say otherwise. As do Martin's."

"I got these punching a wall."

"Darren, lying to the police is not a good move. There were witnesses. Do yourself a favour and give your own side."

He leaned forward on the table and glared at her. "I didn't do it." His voice was rough and his breath stank.

Shona, taking it in her stride, also leant forward. "I've several witnesses." She leant back in her chair, folded her arms, looked him in the eye and said, "I'm giving you one last chance before I arrest you for obstructing a police officer in the course of their duty."

The sound of rusty cogs turning was almost palpable. Darren's brain wasn't used to working out complex problems like this. Shona was happy to let him think. She settled back in her chair.

Darren decided this wasn't going to go away. "We did have a fight, but it was justified."

"So why did you lie?"

"You lot of tossers are probably just waiting for an excuse to arrest me for the murder. Case closed. Never mind I didn't do it."

"Of course we're not. We're more likely to think you did it if you lie through your teeth. What was the argument about?"

"Martin was doing the dirty on Sarah."

Shona looked at Nina who responded, "Sarah Martrand, Ma'am. The deceased's girlfriend."

"Who was he doing the dirty with?"

"Who wasn't he? He was a serial lech. Only got away with it because Felix thinks he walks on water. Felix's wife was probably the only totty he wasn't drilling."

"Mr Spottiswood I do not like your turn of phrase."

"What is this, a convent?"

"No it's my nick and what I say goes. Clean up your act."

"Pussy."

Shona was halfway to Darren's throat when Nina grabbed her and dragged her back.

"You attacked my client."

Shona smoothed down her dress. "I never touched him. He's jolly lucky I didn't though or he'd be joining his oppo in the morgue."

"Are you threatening my client?"

"Oh shut up. He's alive and kicking isn't he? He'll still be able to pay you."

McCluskey's look said Shona was for the high jump. She'd have to deal with that later.

She shoved a sheet of paper and pen over to Spottiswood. "Write down the names of everyone you know he was sleeping with. Your lawyer can help you."

"I had to get out of there. This case is doing my head in. I'd rather have the Alexeyev twins and Pa Broon than this lot."

"Be careful what you wish for, Ma'am. Can we just shove them all in the River Tay and be done with it?"

"Feel free. I'll provide an alibi."

Shona gave herself a few minutes to calm down and went back into the interview room. Darren handed over the paper. There were about ten names on it. Martin had been a busy boy.

"Where were you last night, Darren?"

"At a wine bar with Sarah."

Martin's girlfriend "What did Martin have to say about this?"

"Nothing to do with him. According to him he was rehearsing his lines. You'll find he was probably with one of the titties on that piece of paper."

"Mr Spottiswood, you have to be one of the most vulgar men I have ever had the misfortune to meet. In this line of business I meet a lot."

Even his lawyer was looking a bit askance. "Darren, if you don't stop referring to women in those terms you can engage a new lawyer."

Shona's jaw dropped so far it was like a lift out of control. *Did McCluskey just tell her client off?* Nina's face mirrored Shona's. That had to be the first time McCluskey had ever agreed with anything they said.

"You can't ditch me. I'm entitled to a lawyer."

"Yes you are. But you are not entitled to me. Find yourself another lawyer."

More jaw dropping. Shona looked at McCluskey who smiled at her. Yes, smiled. Okay it was more like the grimace of a Rottweiler but it was something. This was turning out to be one strange day.

"Interview ended at 15.45 to allow Darren Spottiswood to engage a new lawyer." That was the first, and probably would be the only, time she had ever said that.

As Margaret rose to leave Shona shook her hand. Another first and a possible new friendship in the making. Maybe that was taking it just a wee bit too far.

Let's say greater respect, she thought.

.

14

By this point Shona was all interviewed out. She was exhausted with the shenanigans of Xavier and his mates all of whom were worse than the Chief. Talking of the Chief, he was back and had murder on his mind. Not the cases but Shona's murder.

"For once I would like to go to a meeting without you turning the whole place into a disaster zone. I've returned to a pile of complaints about you."

"Complaints, Sir? Complaints plural? I didn't think I'd upset that many people."

"Don't be so insolent Inspector."

Shona stood up a bit straighter and looked him in the eye. "I'm not trying to be insolent, Sir, but the only upset person I'm aware of is Louis Starkind."

"Let's take him first. What gave you the impression it was all right to be rude to one of the most illustrious actors of our time?"

"That's not fair, Sir. I was actually quite polite to him."

"It's the quite I'm worried about. What did you say?"

"Nothing, Sir. I was honestly biting my lip. He took the hump over nothing."

"I'll give you the benefit of the doubt this time. Just keep away from him."

"That will be difficult given I'm investigating his son's murder."

"If we need to speak to him I will do it. Now that brings me to Ex Lord Provost Brown."

"Pa Broon? What's he got to do with this?" Shona's voice rose several decibels. She couldn't seem to move for the Ex Lord Provost. Power mad and despotic he held Dundee tightly in his very wealthy grip.

"He has invested a lot of money in this film production. He has put in a complaint that you are holding up filming."

"I'm investigating a murder. I've better things to worry me than Pa Broon's finances."

"Inspector, you will treat me and the Ex Lord Provost with respect."

"Sorry, Sir." The surliness in her voice gave lie to her words.

"Sort this out as quickly as possible and keep the Ex Lord Provost updated."

"Not a chance," she said staring at her feet.

"What did you say?"

"I said, he'll lead me a merry dance."

"I am sure he will. That is no excuse for you to retaliate. Consider yourself warned."

She left, thinking fondly of how nice it would be to find his rotting corpse in a wood. This cheered her up so much she was grinning when she entered the main office.

She opened her mouth to speak just as the desk sergeant puffed his way through the door. He looked a bit blue about the lips.

"You're not looking so good, Sergeant. Shall I get help?"

"I'm okay. Just a wee bit puffed out. We need a lift in this place." The slap of buttocks hitting chair seat reverberated throughout the room.

"How can I help you?" *If he doesn't give up smoking that chest of his is going to help him shuffle of the earth.*

"There was a young lassie and laddie waiting to see you. They both wanted to talk to the officer in charge of the case."

"Did you say *was* waiting?"

"I did, Ma'am. You've been that busy I couldn't slip them in. They're both coming back in the morning."

"Any clue as to what it might be about?"

"Said they had information for you."

Shona bit her cheek hard to stop shouting at the man. "What time?" Her tone, indicative of her annoyance, was sharper than she would have liked. She didn't care. How was she meant to undertake an investigation with witnesses who were AWOL?

"Nine thirty. After your press conference."

An excuse to cut the press off when they got too annoying. Clouds and silver linings and all that. Shona rapidly forgave the man his transgressions. Time to knock off for the night. She was the first one out of the door, the others left trailing in her wake.

On the way to meet Douglas Shona took a detour to Ninewells Hospital. She'd give Mo, the cleaner, her card and show a bit of solidarity. For once she parked in the car park and divvied up her money for parking. Ten minutes walking down interminable corridors and down several flights of stairs to subterranean levels took her to the correct ward. From the look of Ernie's grey face, closed eyes and laboured breathing, he was not long for this world. Mo burst into tears at the sight of Shona, who found herself trapped between Mo's enormous breasts in a voluptuous hug. Once she'd struggled free she asked how Ernie was doing. She had been right. Ernie would be meeting his maker before the night was out.

"He's going to a better place, Shona. My Ernie knows he's going to heaven."

"That's good to hear, Mo. If you need anything you just let me know. Anything. Remember."

"You're a good lassie, Shona. You've a good heart."

I wish she'd tell the Chief that. He thinks I'm Attila the Hun.

"We're all thinking of you, Mo. You're part of the family." As Shona left they both had tears in their eyes.

For once Shona and Douglas were able to have a date that didn't involve a dead body or his kids. They both loved their work, and Rory and Alice, but it was nice to have a break from both. Some adult time was badly needed. He took her to a swanky new restaurant. All starched linen and intimate candles it served French cuisine. This meant nice food in mouse-size portions. Shona didn't care. She was happy anywhere as long as she was with Douglas. Candlelight flickered throwing soft shadows over her face. As the surroundings and Douglas's blue eyes soothed her, she relaxed into the evening and their relationship. As he reached for her hand all thoughts of murder flew from her mind.

15

Murderous thoughts returned, and peace flew out the door, the minute she entered the Gulags the next morning. Thoughts of reporters had her reaching for a gun. To shoot herself or the first reporter who asked a stupid question, she wasn't quite sure? She'd dressed for the occasion in a short peach dress that highlighted her tan. Her mantra: if you are going to be in the papers, you might as well look good. Plus, from previous experience the *BBC* and *STV* would be camped on her doorstep as well as the print editions of all national and local press.

By nine o'clock she'd made a dent in the paper mountain on her desk and downed three mugs of rocket loaded coffee. She was wired and ready to take no prisoners. Luckily for her reputation and career the Chief informed her he would be taking the conference. She would tag along. The Chief liked his moment in the limelight. However, he couldn't be seen to shove aside the officer in charge of the case. His compromise usually meant he did the talking and left her to field awkward questions. Then, if anything went wrong, it was her fault. No one could fault his logic. His logic left Shona plotting his demise.

Whatever Shona said about the Chief she had to admire his skill at press conferences. A five-minute overview, telling them everything and yet nothing, and the Chief was heading back to his office. It was pure genius. He left Shona dealing with total bedlam. The room had erupted when Martin Crook-Statham's name had been mentioned. His star status was NEWS of the *Hear all About it* variety. His cinematic experience guaranteed this. Well, his geneology at least. The barrage of questions nearly blew Shona back out the door.

"What is Louis Starkind saying about his son's murder?"

"That he is devastated. He will give the police all the assistance they need to solve his murder." Shona had her fingers crossed behind her back at this point. She was also praying it didn't come back to haunt her.

"Adanna Okifor, *Dundee Courier*. Do you think the cases are linked?"

"It is too early to speculate as to any relationship between them. However, we will be doing all we can to find out."

"Surely you must have some idea?"

"Are you deaf? I said we don't know." She took a deep breath. "Any sensible questions?"

"*BBC News*. Do you think the remaining members of the film crew are safe? Could this be someone with a grudge against them?"

More bedlam. She gave it a few minutes and then said loudly and clearly into the mike, "Can we have some quiet please?" The dull roar fell to a gentle murmur. "We have no reason to believe that this is not a murder, singular. That will be all."

As she walked from the room she met Peter. He'd been standing outside listening. "Probably not a sensible thing to say, Ma'am. With your track record it could come back to haunt you."

"Don't you start. You read too many of those rags. You're beginning to sound like them."

"They're no ra—"

"Whatever."

Shona was astonished to find the young man and

Chinese woman from the previous day slouched in chairs and waiting for her. These were the laddie and lassie the Sergeant had referred to. How long had the poor souls sat around yesterday before the Sergeant sent them packing?

She stopped beside them.

"DI Shona McKenzie. I'm sorry for your wait. I believe you wanted to speak to me. If you'd both like to come to the interview room we can get started."

It was a little chaotic in the interview room. Neither wanted to speak. It took Shona a few minutes to realise they had come separately not as a pair. The young man indicated the lady should go first. He, and his earphones, returned to the waiting room.

"How may I help you Miss…?"

"Zhou."

May I have your first name?"

"Miriam." The words were heavily accented.

"How can I help you?'

"Speak English not good."

Fortuitously it turned out the girl was a Cantonese speaker. Abigail was summoned and appeared promptly.

"Your Chinese language skills are needed."

Rapid conversation ebbed and flowed for what seemed like hours. Shona's romantic date had seen her return to her flat at 2 am. Her head started to nod and she jerked it upright. Her eyes started to close but shot open when she heard Abigail call her.

"Ma'am. Ma'am."

Shona pulled herself upright and managed to focus on Abigail.

"Miriam thinks the corpse in the wood might belong to her father."

"How does she even know about the dead body in

the wood? She was here yesterday when we barely knew ourselves?"

Nina turned back to the girl and the sing song language recommenced.

Shona's eyebrows almost met her hairline as she strained to keep her eyes open.

Eventually, "She's the girlfriend of one of the PCss. He phoned and told her they'd found a body. Her dad's been missing for eight months."

Shona gritted her teeth until her jaw hurt.

"Why does she think this person may be her father?"

More rapid chat.

"He was over visiting from China. They live in Hong Kong. It's a city and overpopulated. He liked to spend time with nature."

"How tall was her father, and how old?"

Rapid Cantonese then, "Five foot six and fifty-three years old."

"Thank her for letting us know. Could she bring in something of her father's such as a hairbrush for DNA profiling? Tell her we will keep her posted with any updates."

Once this had been explained Shona stood up. She pulled Abigail aside and said, "Get the boyfriend's name. He's going to be re-evaluating his future in Police Scotland."

She got up to leave and then paused. She sat down again, switched on the tape and did the preliminaries. "What does her father do for a living?"

When Abigail turned back to Shona her usually inscrutable face was one round O! "He was a movie producer."

Shona just about held on to her professional integrity and kept her face sombre.

"Did he have anything to do with the shower down

at Discovery Point?"

"The answer was yes. He had invested some money in the company."

Bingo, they had a link. Maybe the victim in the wood was Mr Zhou.

The laddie turned out to be Jay Dorman, a law student and ultra-marathon runner. This explained why he always looked like a half-shut knife. Exhaustion did that to a person.

"My sergeant tells me you have some information for me."

"It might be nothing but I thought I'd come anyway."

"Always the best option. Let us decide if it's nothing."

"I don't want to waste your time."

You're wasting my flaming time with all this shilly-shallying. Spit it out already.

"Please, what have you got for us?"

I swear that one more minute of this politeness and I'll reach my boiling point. Shona shuffled in her chair. She rubbed her knee, which was feeling the effects of her morning run.

"I was running along Riverside the night that body was found."

All thoughts of knee and pain forgotten Shona leaned forward. "What did you see?"

"I passed a cloaked figure. He was walking close to the wall."

Shona thought fast. There was a low stone wall running the full length of Riverside along the River Tay.

"Did you see where he went?"

'Nah, I was long gone. Training for my next ultra."

"What time was this?"

"About 4 am. I had to finish an assignment before I could escape for a run."

"Can you give us any more details about the person such as height build, hair colour?"

"You having a laugh? I was pounding the pavement at top speed. I wouldn't have noticed him at all if he wasn't wearing a cloak."

"Don't get snippy with me. What makes you think it was a man?"

"Short hair as far as I could tell."

"Could it have been a woman?"

"Possibly. I'm not into gender analysis. Can I go? I've a lecture I have to get to. It's one of the must-do ones."

This bloke could get a place in McCluskey and Runcie. He could be the spawn of the slimy pair. If they weren't brother and sister that is. I wonder if they're related?

Using all the willpower she had not to strangle him she merely said, "That will be all. Leave all your details with the desk sergeant. We'll be in touch if we need you."

The main office was strangely quiet and Shona was a couple of officers short of a full complement.

"Where have Iain and Jason gone?"

"Its no' where they've gone it's where they are. Not reported for duty yet."

"What?"

"They were out on the lash last night." Roy's face was modelling the smug look.

"How come you managed to get in? You're not drunk are you?" She didn't really think this was the case but with Roy it was always best to check.

"I didn't go out."

"What? Two shocks in quick succession are a bit

much for me."

"I'm all mature now. I've got a flat and a toaster and all that sort of stuff. You know, all the grown-up things."

Shona and all three Sergeants were stunned into silence.

"Did you say mature and grown-up in the same sentence? That sentence where you're talking about yourself?" The weakness of Shona's voice was unusual.

"Yep."

More stunned silence until Peter said, "I've called the other pair in. Do you want to deal with them or shall I do it?"

"Over to you. I might kill them and it's bad for my career." She walked over to Roy's desk. "I need you to do a search on a Mr Zhou Yang. Lives in Hong Kong. Went missing eight months ago in UK."

She called over to Abigail. "Get on HOLMES. Do a missing persons search. Time period six to eight months ago."

"Nina, you and I are off to see Mary and then we're going to the pub."

"Awesome."

"Not a drop will pass our lips."

"Bummer. A nice cold Bud would have slipped down nicely."

"Peter, when our drunk duo appear find something suitably horrible for them to do. Preferably something that will make them feel nauseous."

"You're a cruel woman, Ma'am."

"That pair are going to find out just how cruel."

Mary's office was an oasis of cool comfort in the midst of the summer heat. They turned down coffee but accepted a coke each.

"Have you got anything for us, Mary?"

"Your man, Jedediah. Definitely death by hanging, but also drugged. Not enough to knock him out I don't think, but enough that he was not quite compos mentis. Both legs shattered. He'd been hit with something heavy and blunt. Repeatedly."

"Sounds like someone wanted revenge. Anything that brutal is usually personal." She thought for a minute. "Hang on, I need to make a quick call."

She pulled out her phone and pressed 3 on speed dial. "Can I speak to Peter?" After a couple of minutes pause, "Have *Dumb and Dumber* appeared?" She listened for a minute. "Awesome. Once they've done that send them to Discovery Point. They can do a full sweep of the area for blood. Also look for anything which might have been used as a blunt instrument. Abigail can go with them."

Pressing end call she said, "I want to know if he was beaten with the blunt instrument in situ or if he was carted there with broken bones."

"Does your brain ever stop, Shona?"

"Not when I've got a case, no."

"That'll be never then, Shona."

"Nina, if you're going to insult me at least call me Ma'am."

Not only did Nina laugh at this remonstration but Mary also joined in. Shona smiled.

Shona shrugged and said, "Have you got anything on our skeletonised corpse in the woods?"

"Nary a thing."

"Any chance you could tell us the victim's height, race and age?"

"You don't ask for much do you? Come on, we'll take a look. The remains are on a table awaiting my tender ministrations."

They kitted up and followed Mary into the morgue. It was as cold as Scott's trip to the Antarctic and they were wearing the thinnest of scrubs. Not a happy combination for the hothouse plant detective. She shivered as she watched Mary confidently carry out her task. Her movements swift she measured and calculated. She talked as she worked. "Humerus 32 cm. multiply that by five, 160 cm." She consulted a chart and her finger moved downward over its surface. "Yep, roughly five foot three inches."

"Could it have been taller?"

She measured from head to toe. "Nope, coming in at 5 feet two inches. The two measurements correlate."

Shona sighed. *Too short for Mr Zhou.* "What about sex and nationality?"

She pointed to the face. "This is rough as I can't say for certain. I'd say the high skull, straight face, and protruding nose indicates Caucasian."

Definitely not Mr Zhou.

"Age and sex?"

"Age, I'd say initially under fifty. Need to run x-rays to get a better idea."

"How do you work that out?" Nina had been uncharacteristically quiet up until now.

Mary pointed at the pelvis. "Symphysis is still zigzag. It straightens out after age fifty. Our skeleton also has the pelvic structure of a female."

"Thanks, Mary. I'll let you get on with the rest of the examination."

"You can pay me back by keeping the corpse count down."

Before Shona could open her mouth, Nina said, "You have got to be kidding. This is Shona we're talking about."

"There is that."

"Shona grabbed Nina's arm and dragged her away. "You've got scutwork written in your future."

"Duly noted, Ma'am." The sound of her laughter

echoed along the empty corridor.

16

The Rabbie was packed as per usual. The Robert Falcon Scott public house bucked the trend of declining punters in pubs. Shona didn't want to enquire too closely into the owner's secret. She might not like the answer and shutting the Rabbie would get her murdered. Or at the very least run out of town. It was too hot to be fleeing from braying mobs.

Alex, the owner, was pulling pints like a maniac. He glanced in their direction and a smile split his leathery face. "Bonnie day, ladies. I'll bet you'd like couple of drinks."

Before Shona could refuse he called over to his young barman. "Cloth-ears. Get Shona and Nina a couple of nice cold nonalcoholic lagers. On the house."

"No, Alex. We must pay."

"Wouldn't hear of it. No officer of the law has ever paid for a drink in my pub. It's my way of thanking you for keeping the streets safe."

Yeah, right. More likely to be bribing us to keep his pub open. She reminded herself to keep an open mind.

"When you've got a minute we need to chat."

"Sienna," he yelled through the door. His teenage granddaughter appeared with a glass-cloth in her hand. "Go fetch your gran. She needs to cover here."

The lass scurried to do his bidding. Shona and Nina squeezed into a corner and took a sip of their beer. It slipped down the throat like honey and lowered the temperature nicely.

"Wicked."

"Wipe your mouth, Nina. You've grown a moustache."

Nina pulled a tissue from her Cartier handbag and

dabbed her lips taking care not to smudge her coral pink lipstick. Shona had no doubt that it was Estee Lauder's most expensive make. Nina was a fashion plate model, with the mind and cunning of a detective. A dastardly duo of personalities.

They'd managed a few mouthfuls before Alex collected them and took them off to a sitting room behind the pub. He chucked a couple of packets of crisps at them. "Mature cheddar for you, Shona and sea salt and cracked black pepper for you, Nina."

The pair pulled the bags open and stuffed a few crisps in their mouth.

"A feast fit for a king," said Shona when she'd swallowed a few of the crisps. She put the packet down on an orange Formica coffee table, not sure if the décor was meant to be shabby chic or was the original seventies furniture. *Either way it's hideous.*

"I believe you've had several of the film crew visiting your establishment."

"Not several, all of them have been cluttering the place up. The regulars can hardly get through the door. I've given them free reign of one of the function suites."

"You don't sound happy."

"The only thing that useless shower is good for is spending money. I've just about doubled my takings since they arrived."

Alex was usually the affable host and loved everyone. His dislike of the film crew was not in his DNA.

"What's up with them then?" She leaned in and spoke in a tone redolent of conspiracy.

"All they do is argue."

"What about?"

"Everything. Every flaming thing. They're also a

bunch of ignorant tossers. Told me my pub did not reflect the high status of Robert Falcon Scott." He assumed a posh English accent for the latter phrase.

Whoops! Shona and Nina glanced at each other, both choking back a smile. Fastest way to upset a publican. Tell him his pub's rubbish. There was no denying the pub was rather scruffy. Pointing this out was not the way to go.

Shona pulled out a photo and waved it in front of his nose. "Has this man been in here?"

He peered at the photo. A couple of years old, it was of Jedediah.

"Do I know him? I'll never forget him. He had wandering hands syndrome. Patted my Sienna's bum. Lech."

Shona's investigative radar sat up straight and begged. "I bet you didn't take that lying down."

"No, I never. I told him if he ever laid a finger on any woman in my family he'd be acting dead, only he wouldn't be acting."

"Alex, you do realise you've just given us a motive for you having murdered Martin?"

"Aye. But I didn't. I've a family to think of. That jumped up little scrote isnae worth me going to jail over."

"Where were you the night of the murder?"

"Up A&E with my lassie's wean. He's three and managed to fall out his brother's top bunk. At 11.30 at night."

Shona tipped her head to Nina, who correctly interpreted it. She wrote down a note to follow that up.

"Thanks. Sorry to hear about your grandson. Can you give me any specifics about the arguments?"

"You've got to be joking. This place is crazy. It takes me all my time to remember the drinks people want. I will say that Dalai Lama lookalike's a bit weird though. Not quite right in the head if you ask me."

"Just because he's a Buddhist doesn't mean he's weird. That's a bit racist."

"I'm no' talking about his religion. He was always deep in conversation with one o' the actors. Not that he did much talking. Just listened."

"He's a religious advisor; that's what they do."

"Yes, but are they meant to be recording everything that's said?"

Shona sat bolt upright. "Did I hear you right?"

"You did. Recorded everything they said. I occasionally saw it through his robes. They were all too busy being deep and meaningful to notice themselves."

"Did you tell them?"

"Nothing to do with me. You see all sorts in here and learn to keep your mouth shut." He took in the look on Shona's face. "Unless I think someone's broken the law that is."

"Going back to Jedediah?"

"Who?"

"Martin, the man who is dead."

"Oh, him. What about him?"

"I want to know more about his status as a lothario."

"You've come to the right man."

17

Her ringing phone stopped Shona before she'd taken two steps outside the door.

"Abigail, how's it going?"

Squeaking from the phone.

"Go for it. I'll square it with the Chief." She hung up and chucked her phone back in her handbag.

"I don't know how you ever find anything in that bag. It's bigger than you." Nina lengthened her stride to keep up with her boss who was marching off into the distance.

"Better than the postage stamp you call a handbag."

"What's the Chief going to get upset about now?"

"Iain, despite his hangover, is doing a cracking job. He's found traces of blood on the wall between the film set and the river."

"And that will upset the Chief, why?"

"Because Abigail thinks the murder weapon may have been heaved over there. We're going to be dredging the river."

"You've just authorised divers. I'm in awe. I'm not sure the Chief will be though. Especially since it could be some daft bat who's cut his or her hand whilst gazing fondly at the water. "

"Let's not worry about trivialities. The Chief will just have to deal with it." Shona's voice held a cheerful note. Not bad for someone who would probably be going to the gallows once she'd spoken to the boss.

They hurried back to the car and switched the engine on. There was a communal sigh as the air conditioning kicked in. Bliss.

When she got back to the office Peter was reading the *Dundee Courier*.

"Gainfully employed, I see."

"Having a wee break. I've been hard at it all morning."

"I shall enjoy hearing about the fruits of your labour."

Roy, head down, was producing smoke from the keyboard.

"What have you got for me, Roy?"

"Eh?"

"Roy, focus. What have you found out about Mr Zhou?"

Roy looked up and sat back in his chair. "An interesting man, Ma'am."

"Interesting as in he's done a lot or interesting as in it will help us?"

"Both."

Shona pulled over a chair and sat down. "Hit me with it."

"International entrepreneur and business man. He's got fingers in every single pie going from food, to newspapers and movies. Came from nothing as he started life as the son of a poor labourer."

"How did he manage to crawl out of poverty and into millionaire status?"

"I haven't managed to figure that out yet but he's not a millionaire. Billionaire would be more accurate. He's the second richest man in the world."

"How come he went missing in Dundee and I've not heard a whisper of him?"

"Looks like he managed to get into the country incognito. Maybe a false passport was involved."

"Don't speculate about his criminal activities. We don't know he has any. Did he come in somewhere on a private jet?" Shona's heart was pounding. Hollywood

stars and a billionaire Chinaman, both connected to a cheapskate movie that was being shot in Dundee. *I mean, Dundee's great and all but not exactly the centre of the Hollywood film industry.*
"I'll look into it."
"I'm off to speak to his daughter. See if she can shed any light."

Shona picked up the phone and dialled Miriam Zhou's mobile. "Miriam, I'm sorry but I need to ask you a few questions."
"Will assist police where I can."
"Why was your father in Scotland?" Shona, remembering the girl's poor grasp of English, kept her questions simple.
"He visit me."
"How did he get here?"
"Excuse. Not understand."
Shona paused. A few seconds then, "I will get my Sergeant to phone you."
She rang Abigail, outlined what she needed, and gave her Miriam's number.

While she was playing the waiting game she went to brief the Chief and break the news about the divers.
"Do whatever is needed. Stop bothering me unless you have a significant breakthrough. You will use everything at your disposal to solve this case immediately."
Shona stood in stunned silence. She'd girded her loins for battle and the easy capitulation had her confused.
"That will be all, Inspector."
Her mind was too much of a whirlwind to even think about plotting his demise.

"Peter, have I missed something? What's the deal with the Chief?"

"Have you no' heard?"

"Obviously not, Peter, or I wouldn't be asking you to explain. Spit it out man."

"The Prime Minister's been on the phone. Seems he and Louis Starkind went to Eton together. Frightfully good friends don't you know." The last part of the sentence was uttered in a mock upper class English accent. It was surprisingly good for someone with an accent like Peter's.

"No wonder the Chief's in a tizzy. This just gets better and better."

"It certainly does, Ma'am. You never fail to entertain and delight with the weirdness of your cases," said Nina.

"Oxford was never as bad as this."

"Dundee always does it better. We're one o' a kind Ma'am." Peter shut his newspaper and folded it neatly. "Do you want an update on what I've been doing?"

"Glad you can spare me the time."

The ringing of a phone interrupted the pleasant exchange. "Abigail. Shoot."

Rapid talking ensued. Shona hung up and shouted across the room. "Roy, Mr Zhou came in on a private jet. It's been parked in Riverside Airport for the last several months. You're losing your touch."

"I wasn't exactly going to hack into Her Majesty's Customs and Excise. It'd be difficult to pay my mortgage from prison."

"You could have phoned them."

She turned back to Peter and Nina. "This brings us to the whereabouts of our Mr Zhou. Now we've a missing person case on our hands and somehow it's tied up with that bunch down at Riverside."

"Did I hear you say at some point, Ma'am, that this

was going to be an easy case?"

"Nina, I said no such thing."

"Aye, Ma'am. You'll find you did."

"Instead of calling out my transgressions you might want to get on and do something about finding Mr Zhou."

.

18

Iain and Jason looked like a couple of half-cooked tattie scones. Beside them Abigail looked both tanned and cheerful. In fact she was stunningly beautiful in a yellow flower print dress.

"It's a bonnie day out there. It makes you glad to be alive and even more glad to be a police officer on location."

She said this loudly whilst standing right next to Jason. He groaned and rubbed his temples.

"You pair, get some aspirin and fluids in you. You've ten minutes before I get a report."

They scurried off.

"Don't even think about a bacon roll," she yelled after them.

Jason hurtled in the direction of the toilets.

"Wasn't that a bit mean, Ma'am?" Abigail's generous nature jumped to the fore.

"Nah, serves the pair of them right."

Before they met in the briefing room she pulled the pair of them aside. No longer jocular, she said, "I know Peter has dealt with you, but I want to add my disappointment. If either of you appear in my, or any other station, in that state again you will be fired. If you are late again you will be removed from my team. Are we clear?"

The pair stared at the parquet flooring.

"I said, are we clear?"

"Yes, Ma'am. Sorry, Ma'am." The words were mumbled in perfect unison.

"There will be a line drawn under this. Your one

and only line."

The boards in the briefing room were beginning to look full. Full but so far not a jot on there that would help them solve the case or cases.

"You go first, Iain. Are you up to the task?"

"Yes, Ma'am." The lad looked less pasty than his partner in crime.

"Take it away."

"We did a full sweep of the area for blood spatter. Small amounts of blood at the back of a pile of crates used as stage props."

"How come we didn't notice this before?'

"The area formed a space between the props and the sea wall. There was a load of other stuff shoved in there. We pulled things out to do a sweep."

"So why not just shove him over the sea wall? With compound fractures of both tibia and fibia there was no way he was swimming to safety."

"I might just have the answer to that," said Roy.

"Go for it Wonderboy."

"One of Scott's Scottish ancestors was hanged by the Jacobites."

"Brilliantly deduced. We'll make a detective out of you yet. The killer was making a statement."

"I think it means the killer was an actor. Staging would be in their DNA," said Abigail.

"Also a good point. Iain, have we got a match with the victim's blood?"

"Not had a chance to take a look."

"Off you go. Get the answer to me soonest."

He bounded off full of energy. His recovery from last night's excesses had obviously been prompt.

"Peter, you said you'd been gainfully employed. What doing?"

"I googled all the actors and put together an

overview of their careers to date." He waved a sheaf of papers in the air. "I added some juicy gossip about them as well."

He took in Shona's face and hurriedly added, "All pertinent of course."

He passed around the sheets of paper.

"Good job, Peter."

Silence ensued as they read his update.

"Our dead man was a more accomplished womaniser than Roy. I didn't think that was possible," said Jason.

"You might not want to be casting aspersions on Roy given your track record this morning. You're right though. Alex, from the Rabbie, said the same."

"Alex knows everything and everyone," said Peter. "He'll be right whatever he says." He glanced down at his notes and adjusted his reading glasses. "Martin's girlfriend seems like a right piece of work. Upped and left everything in Cornwall to follow him and the movie to Dundee."

"Get her in. Anyone who does that to a lothario love rat must be fixated. I'm sure his womanising must have riled her."

"Riled her enough to kill though?"

"Who knows? Some woman once ran her husband's lover over with a Land Rover. Five times. I don't think she was very impressed."

"Smashing and hanging seems a wee bit out there though. Although I could understand it if she chopped his nuts off."

"Nina! That is quite enough."

The men hurriedly grabbed their nether regions. Shona took in their pained faces and laughed.

"Boys, you're fine. No chopping will be done on my watch. Carry on Peter."

"Our Xavier's been bankrupt a couple of times.

Always manages to crawl out o' the gutter somehow. Word on the street is he knows some influential people."

"And who might they be?"

"No one's saying. Not anywhere I can search anyway."

"Roy. Find that out. Also do a thorough search on Hui Chao the monk. Seems he was recording all the conversations he had with the members of the film crew. Find out about Xavier's current finances."

"Not more of the religious community? Seriously, Ma'am, the ecclesiastical fraternity already thinks you've something against them," said Nina. "Even I'm beginning to think it's a bit suspicious."

"Keep your observations for someone who's interested." Shona's tone was light. Nina recognised the underlying steel.

"Can I use means fair or foul to get the juicy details?"

"Start with fair and I'll get you a warrant to cover the foul."

"I'm on it." He rushed from the room.

"Jason, get Sarah Martrand, the deceased's girlfriend, in. You and Nina can interview her." She pulled a packet of mints from her pocket and threw them at him. "Here, chew on these. You smell like a brewery following a stag night."

She was downing her second cup of freshly brewed coffee when a small tornado flew through her door. The tornado was accompanied by a very bouncy King Charles spaniel puppy.

"Alice. How lovely to see you."

The puppy hurled itself at Shona, jumped on her lap and started licking her face.

"Charlie, down."

The puppy stared at her then returned to the licking.

Shona lifted the puppy down and gently placed him on the floor. One hand firmly held him there. "Alice, what brings you here? In fact, who brought you here? I know for a fact that your father's in court." Alice Lawson was Douglas's daughter.

"Me and Rory were out walking Charlie. We thought we'd come and see you."

"You shouldn't really be bringing dogs in here."

"That's not fair. Fagin's always in here."

The girl had a point. "That's different. He's the station mascot."

A pout appeared but the girl's sunny nature won out. "Rory and me want you to come for tea. Dad says we can have pizza."

"I'll see what I can do. Don't eat all the pizza, mind, if I'm late."

"No way I'm promisin' you that. Bye Shona. I'm going to see if Uncle Peter has cake."

The tornado and the puppy departed. Shona hurtled after them. "You can't run around here on your own."

"You talking to yourself, Ma'am? I've got Sarah Martrand in interview room one."

"Thanks Jason. Grab Abigail and do the interview between you. Do you feel up to it?"

"Absolutely, Ma'am. No way I'll let you down."

"Best see you don't."

Shona found Rory. "You can't let your sister run around the station unaccompanied."

"Can you keep her and the Hound of the Baskervilles under control?"

"That's not the point. Go find her and stay with her."

A good-natured soul, the lad nodded and wandered off. He too wandered in the direction of Peter and the cake.

Peter was nowhere to be seen in the office. Roy, on the other hand, was present and hard at it. Shona was amazed at how he'd settled down. In the past there had been several instances where he nearly returned to uniform. Now he seemed to be embracing his mature side. It probably wouldn't last long but she'd take it where she could get it.

"What's the dark web brought us?"

"Enough to keep us going for a couple of months."

"Great. Who'd have thought a bunch of two-bit thespians would be so much trouble."

"Well, let me tell—"

Jason crashed through the door and said, "You need to be in the interview with her, Ma'am. Her brother's here and he's not best pleased."

"What's it got to do with him?"

"He's also her lawyer."

"Why me, Lord?"

19

"Interview with Sarah Martrand. Also present her lawyer, Shane Martrand, DI Shona McKenzie and Jason Roberts." She'd given Abigail her marching orders as the interview room was beginning to look like a department store in the sales.

The brother had a Welsh accent so thick you'd need an axe to cut it.

"I've come all the way from Llantwit."

"Sorry, did you say you came from Clan Twit?" Puzzlement leapt from Shona's eyes.

"You stupid woman. Llantwit. L L A N T W I T. Can't you speak the language the good Lord gave us?"

"My Welsh is a little rusty. There is no need to shout."

She could hear muttering beside her. "I'd like to hear him tryin' to speak Scottish."

She turned and glared at Jason. Then took in Sarah. The girl was wearing jeans that must have been sprayed on, and a voluminous purple and green tie-dyed dress.

"Miss Martrand, thank you for coming in. I believe you were Jedediah's girlfriend?"

"No. I was Martin's girlfriend. Who's Jede whatsit?"

"Martin's real name was Jedediah Ramsbottom."

"You're crazy. Why are you making things up about him?"

"No one's making anything up. How long had you been going out with Jeded..." She took in the girl's tear-filled eyes. "Martin?"

"Three months."

"You gave up everything to follow him here and

you barely knew him?"

"We were soulmates. Destined to be together."

"Rubbish, Sarah. Mam and Dad told you he was no good. You made a right show of them coming here."

"Mr Martrand that's enough. By the way, where did you study law?"

"You can't ask me that. It's immaterial."

"Yes I can. This is Scotland and it's Scots law here. So unless you studied law in Scotland you're no use to us."

"I studied in Cardiff."

"Then can you please leave?"

"What? I'm supporting my sister. You can't throw me out."

"Your sister is an adult. She doesn't need supporting. Support her in silence or sling your hook."

"Preposterous."

"Do you know the meaning of silence?" She glared at him and his teeth clenched. The look in his eyes said there would be a lawsuit landing on her desk.

"So you were destined to be with a man and you didn't know his name?"

The tears reappeared. They were wasted on Shona who continued, "It would seem that you weren't the only string to Martin's bow."

"What are you talking about?"

"I've heard that he had several women on the go."

"That's not true. Take that back."

Shona lifted up a sheet of paper. She read from the list, "Dionne Perlman, Amanda Jeffries, Zoe Gillespie, Jean Barrister, Leanne Morris—"

Sarah had her hands over her ears. "Stop it. Stop it. You're a lying pig." She started to cry.

Her brother jumped up. "Stop bullying her. This is outrageous."

"I'm not bullying her. The man was a serial

womaniser."

"Don't you think I know tha...?" He stopped as he realised what he had just said.

"PC Roberts, please find Sergeants Johnston and Chakrabarti. They can escort Mr Martrand to Interview Room 2."

When the pair appeared Shona took them outside and brought them up to date with what had happened. "Interview him till he's round about and upside down. Find out where he was on the night in question."

Shona returned to her interview. "Where were you the night Martin was killed? I would have thought two people so much in love would have been together."

"Martin had lines to learn. He could not be disturbed when his inner thespian was calling."

"So what were you up to?"

"I was with Stephen."

"Who's Stephen?"

"Martin's understudy. A real gentleman. We've become such precious friends over the last few weeks."

Wasn't he interviewed a couple of days ago? I never did hear the outcome.

"Ma'am, I've had a bellyful of interviews. If I've got to speak to any more jumped-up Luvvies I'm going to sign out a gun and shoot myself with it."

"Can I have it after you? Your nearest and dearest need you so off the lot of you go. Iain, I want an update on samples etc. first thing in the morning."

She contemplated going to Douglas's house and spending the evening with him and the kids. Exhaustion and common sense won out. She needed every atom of energy she possessed to get through this case. Besides she had a cat waiting for her at home. She was spending so much time with Douglas that Shakespeare was not best pleased. Shona thought that she might return home one night and there would be a re-creation of the scene with her ex-husband. The cat would be sat at the door with the feline equivalent of Louis Vuittons packed at her feet. Shona would then be left home alone once more.

20

The figure watched as the blood drained from the body. Pooling initially, it slowly soaked into the dry ground, watering the grass with its sticky sweetness. Transferring life from human to nature. Returning from whence it came. Ashes to ashes, dust to dust.

The injured woman's cries were strong at first then grew weaker with each heartbeat as the blood pulsed out of her body. There was no one to hear her pleading, her screams, and her whispers, her whimpering. No one to take note of the silence that followed.

 Her hands tried to stem the flow, an impossible task. She struggled, went limp and took her last weary breath. The life faded from eyes that now stared upwards in death.

The figure stood quietly and waited until death was certain. Then, they crouched over the body and performed one final act. This done, the figure stood up. The heavy cloak swung as they turned and walked away, confident that no one had seen. How could they in this barren spot?

21

The update was not to be. Neither was the morning alarm or breakfast. What she got was a cat with attitude and a body dumped at the top of Auchterhouse Hill. Five o'clock found her shoving on the Tassimo and spooning food into the cat's chipped dish. She'd bought a new one but Shakespeare was having none of it. Refused to eat out of anything other than old faithful. A creature of habit she was capable of going on a hunger strike for weeks should the new stoneware be forced upon her. She dumped the bowl down on the black and white ceramic tiles of the kitchen floor.

"Stop moaning. I'm not getting any breakfast."

Shakespeare's look said, "Who cares?"

A cold shower to cool down and she was out of the door with the coffee in a thermal travel mug. Shona was of the mind these were man's greatest invention.

She had to abandon the car halfway to her destination. The mug was in her hand as she strode the rest of the way. In a red summer frock and pink wellies she felt like a right prat. Her usual footwear didn't have the chutzpah for a walk up a Scottish hill. Sandals didn't go well with rocks and hummocks of grass. Thus was the life of an officer in Police Scotland. She was comforted by the fact that everyone else, apart from Nina, would be similarly attired. Nina would tip up in pair of Christian Louboutin with a matching handbag. She'd look like a million dollars and wouldn't trip over anything.

The POLSA was nowhere to be seen and there was a

fresh faced new bobby guarding the entrance to the crime scene.

"You can't go in there. No poking your nose in. Go back down the hill please."

Shona beamed at him. "DI Shona McKenzie, the officer in charge of the case."

He stared back at her. "Do you have any ID?"

Her hand went to her pocket before realising she didn't have any. Still in her handbag in the car.

Thankfully one of his friends hurried over. "John, let her in. It's DI McKenzie. The legend herself."

The young cop's face went red. "Sorry, Ma'am."

"No need to apologise. You did well. Can I get in please?"

He pulled at the crime scene tape and ushered her through. She hurried over to the body, all the while watching her feet. Going her length on a Scottish hillside would not lend gravitas and professionalism to her day.

The corpse was that of a woman of about twenty-eight, with brassy blonde hair. She had makeup perfectly applied to one side of her face. The other was covered by a large strawberry naevus or birthmark. Her fluffy, light brown jacket and the way she was sprawled gave her the look of a discarded teddy bear. If teddy bears bled that is. The front of the jacket was stained darker brown which was likely indicative of the way she died. That and the knife in the middle of her chest.

A lone tree, gnarled and bent to the vagaries of the constant Scottish wind, stood guard. Peter stood beside it like a faithful companion.

"Are the others on their way?"

"Jason's in his car. I told him to wait there. The others are on their way. Roy's moved to Carnoustie so it'll take him a wee big longer."

"Fair enough. Police Surgeon?"

"On her way. She still lives in Perth."

"So we stand around sunbathing whilst the others take their own sweet time?"

"That's about right." He pulled a packet of mints from his pocket and offered one to Shona.

She took one, unwrapped it and popped it in her mouth. She was regretting not stopping for breakfast.

They gazed around them. The hilltop was barren apart from the tree. Not exactly a lot of cover for hiding anything.

"Why here?" said Shona.

"No' many people come here in the middle o' the night I suppose."

"Still it must have been a struggle for anyone to get a body up here."

"It's pretty steep." Peter rubbed his chest.

"What's up with you?"

"Indigestion. Bolted down a couple of cheese and jam rolls in the car."

"Your wife will have a fit." She fixed a steely gaze on his chest. "And you'll have a heart attack."

"Jeez, Shona. What are you wishing on me?"

She was saved from a reply by Whitney appearing over the top of the hill. Dressed in running shorts, vest and shocking pink running shoes she looked and acted like a jumpy whippet.

"Morning, Shona. I hear you've something for me. Sorry about the attire. I was out running when the call came through. Diverted here so you could get started." She was expertly checking the body over for signs of life.

"Certified dead. I would say the knife wound gives the game away as to probable cause of death. Best not speculate though." She jotted her findings down on a form, tore it from the notepad and handed it to Shona. "Over to you." With that the whirlwind whirled round and headed in the direction of the road.

"That woman exhausts me. Can she no' walk?"

"I'm a runner and she exhausts me."

The rest of the team was present and correct. Apart from Roy, who was apparently caught up in a smash on the Kingsway. He wasn't in the smash just stopped to help until traffic and an ambulance arrived. Iain had his camera out and was clicking like a maniac. Nina had organised the others into a search party and were looking for clues.

"Does she look familiar to you, Peter?"

"Nope. Never seen her before."

"I get the feeling I've seen her. Not sure where though." She thought for a minute. Memories flickered around in her brain, tickling her hippocampus and encouraging it to wake up. Nope. Nothing. Her hippocampus remained unconscious.

"I can't think."

She crouched down and examined the girl more closely. The skin on one side of her face was beautiful. Not a flaw to be seen. The other a mangled mess of blood vessels. Her blue eyes would have been mesmerizing in life. Now they stared heavenwards, unseeing. She picked up the woman's hand and admired the delicacy. Small, slim fingers which had not seen any heavy labour. Nicotine stains indicated she was a smoker. Shona pulled back the lips. No nicotine stains on the teeth. They were white and in two perfect rows. The woman spent money on dental treatment then. So not poor. Shona moved back to the hands. There was something under the fingernails.

"Iain. Swab please."

She swabbed under the nails, popped the evidence in a bag, and sealed it tightly. "Peter, take this to the POLSA. Get it squared away and recorded."

Despite the sunny day the wind whistled across the

hillside adding a greater chill to the scene. Beauty and the beast meet in the most macabre of ways.

She joined the search party but they hunted in vain. The rock strewn hillside, keeping its secrets to itself, yielded nothing. Shona wondered just how many secrets the hill could tell. Was there anything in its past which would concern their future? After a couple of hours of concentrated peering at the ground she knocked it on the head. Uniform had joined in to help them and every blade of grass and stone had been examined in detail.

"It's too dry to get anything here. Iain, have you got all the photos you need?"

"All done here."

"All back to Bell Street. My team anyway." The team trooped off. She turned to the others.

"Thanks for your help guys. You've been troopers. Go and see what Sergeant Muir has for you."

Murmuring, they headed in the direction of the POLSA.

22

For once the Gulags of Bell Street were a welcoming sight. There was a canteen within its walls and Shona intended making full use of it. One mint does not a breakfast make. She'd no sooner sat down than the others joined her. Including Peter who had a full Scottish.

"Peter you've already had breakfast. Seriously. Your wife is going to throw you out."

"It's all grilled. No' a thing in it that'll make me put on weight."

Shona left him to it and tucked into her own full-cooked while it was still hot.

Fully fortified they transported themselves to the briefing room.

"Anyone recognise our latest victim?"

Blank looks all round provided her only answer.

"Soldier Boy, when we're done here you and Roy can go and visit Xavier. Take a photo of the victim and see if she's anything to do with the shower down at the Discovery."

"Was there anything at all found up Auchterhouse Hill?"

"The ground's baked hard as pottery, Ma'am, and the terrain's all scrub and rocks. Not the perfect conditions for evidence."

"Thanks, Iain. I was hoping for something a bit more encouraging."

"We could make something up if it'll make you feel better, Ma'am?"

"Very witty, Abigail. The truth will suffice."

"We'll try and get an identity and go from there."

"Iain, the results from the blood spatters at the crime scene. Have you got them?"

"Yep. Definitely Jedediah's. The stuff on the top of the wall was his as well."

"So your hunch was right, Abigail. Any word back from the divers yet?"

"Nope. I'll give them a ring and see how it's going."

"It's no' going very well. It says so in *The Courier.*"

"How come the newspapers know more about my cases than I do?"

"Because they've had somebody parked down there since it happened. Actors being bumped off are big news."

"You'd think there'd be something more juicy come along by now."

"There is. Our latest victim. The press was sniffing round as I left," Nina chipped in.

Shona rolled her eyes. "Abigail, grab someone from the divers and get a sitrep. Do it now."

Abigail jumped up and trotted off.

"Roy, what's the deepest, darkest, web given us?"

"You'll love this one." He paused.

"Spit it out man. We're dying of old age here."

"Our monk isn't a monk..." Another dramatic pause.

"Roy, I swear..."

"He's a con artist from Glasgow."

The place erupted.

"Quiet." No one heard. Louder. "Will you all shut up?"

They all looked at her round-eyed.

"For heaven's sake. Sometimes I think I'm

working in a nursery. Get a grip."

'Well, you have to admit it's a strange turn of events, Ma'am."

"Peter, we're police officers. We should be able to cope with something different."

"Con artist spiritual advisors are a new one even for us," said Nina.

"Get Hui Chao in. Actually, is that really his name?"

"Of course not. His name's Harry Springer," said Roy.

"It's a frightfully English name for someone who looks Thai. Or for anyone from Glasgow for that matter."

"His mother was Thai. His father was a full-time boxer and part-time safe-cracker. Ended up in Barlinnie for killing a couple of blokes with his bare hands."

"Cheery family. Did you find this out on the net? Was it legal?"

"Yep. Sure did. And it was vaguely legal."

"I'll live with that. Nina, when we're done here get Harry in for questioning. No, strike that. You and I can go and find him."

"Next up is our famed director, Xavier Lovelady."

"Is that really his name?"

"It really is. The only one of them who hasn't changed it."

"What a bloo... bloomin' awful name to saddle a wean with."

"You're right. With a name like that he was destined to land in his chosen career."

"Not exactly a dustman's name."

"Jason, that's quite enough. Our refuse collectors do not deserve to be named in the same sentence as Lovelady."

Loud cheering erupted and Shona took a bow. "Thank you, you've been a great audience."

She waited for everyone to settle down. "Carry on, Roy."

"Lovelady's finances are in dire straits again. He's taken out some huge lump sums recently. There doesn't seem to be any rhyme nor reason to them."

"Are you thinking blackmail?"

"I'm not thinking anything. Neither will you when I give you my next tidbit."

"Roy, are you trying to kill us all off? We've enough suspense without you adding to it."

"Xavier's powerful friends are…"

"Roy, this is not a reality TV show. Give us the information."

"The Alexeyev twins."

Shona took a moment to let this sink in and then jumped up. Her hands shook. "What? Are you telling me the Dundee Mafia - Stephan and Gregor - are bankrolling Xavier Lovelady?"

"I'm not quite sure whether they were bankrolling him, using violence to change debt collectors' minds, or both."

"Get that pair in here." She took in the look on her team's faces. "I don't want any guff about them not coming quietly. You are police officers, so act like them. I don't care how you get them in here, just do it. Peter, get it sorted."

"Aye, don't you fret. They'll be here nice and cosy waiting for you when you get back from speaking to Harry."

The news from the divers was a negative in having found anything yet. However, they hadn't given up. They were trawling the Tay and having a jolly nice time while they did it. Bonny weather and diving were a grand way to spend a day.

Harry lived in a flat above a pub in town. Nina rapped on the peeling brown door. No answer, so she repeated it but with more vigour.

A dull voice could just about be heard from the inner sanctum. "Stop battering the door. I'm coming."

When the door opened Harry stood blinking in front of them, wearing nothing but a string vest and a pair of Superman boxers.

"Aren't you a bit old for Superman?"

"What do you pair want?"

"That's not very nice. I thought monks were hospitable people. Aren't you going to invite us in?"

He yanked back the door and let them walk in. "Go through to the living room."

The living room was a shamble. Widely-strewn clothes, and the remains of the previous evening's curry, lent the room an uncared-for look. Shona and Nina tipped some clothes off a couple of hard-backed chairs and sat down.

After about ten minutes of them staring at the bombsite, Harry reappeared. He was wearing his saffron monk's outfit.

"How can I help you ladies?"

"You can start by getting rid of the recorder."

His face blanched and fear flashed for a brief moment in his eyes. He recovered in the space of a heartbeat. "I don't know what you mean."

"Then you must be thicker than I thought. I've a device on me that can search for anything making a digital recording. So, do yourself a favour and hand it over."

She was lying through her teeth - but why confuse the issue with the facts?

Keeping his face enigmatic he reached inside his robe and pulled out a Dictaphone. He held it firmly and his gaze fixed on Shona.

"I would like you to give it to me."

"I have no intention of doing so. There is confidential information on this."

"I'm absolutely sure of it. It's the confidential information I require."

"I'm not handing this over without a warrant. The information on here is delicate. It would be a breach of trust if I handed it to you."

"Your information was gained illegally. You have to have permission to record someone."

"I'm not handing it over. You don't know what's on it so you can't make me."

"You're right, I can't."

Shona turned and whispered in Nina's ear.

Nina leapt to her feet. "Just got to make a phone call."

Shona switched on her own recorder. "So let's leave that aside and move on to your name. Hui Chao. Is that right?"

His eyes looked everywhere but at Shona. He seemed fascinated by a large crack in the wall just over her shoulder.

"You know it is."

"Does the name Harry Springer mean anything to you?"

Harry leapt from the chair, a look of pure evil on his face. He took a couple of steps closer to Shona who stood up and said, "You may want to rethink your next move."

He stopped and said, "I changed my name legally."

Nina strolled through the door. She stopped short and took in the scene.

"You okay, Ma'am?"

110

"I'm fine." Her eyes didn't move from Harry's. "Your name change doesn't mean you've changed your personality. You're a con artist, pure and simple."

"I've reformed."

"Reformed so much that you're suddenly recording private conversations. Are you blackmailing the members of Pink Play Productions?"

"No. No. You've got it all wrong. I was recording them so I could get better at what I was doing."

"Blackmail?"

"Counselling. I was improving my counselling skills you stupid woman."

"Don't you shout at the Inspector. Keep it civil, chum." She turned her back on Harry and muttered, "We've got the go ahead."

"Harry, we need you to come down to the station with us. Bring the recording device."

"Why? I've done nothing."

"You and half of Dundee. Get a move on we've not got all day."

"You'd better not put me in handcuffs."

"Don't be so dramatic. We only want to ask a few questions. We're taking you to the station so you don't jump ship."

"That was quite good, Ma'am."

"I thought so."

23

The Alexeyevs were awaiting her return to the station. Unfortunately, they were not waiting patiently. Their Slavic tempers, never cowering wee beasties at the best of times, were in full-blown roaring dragon mode today.

"Will you pair shut up?" bellowed Shona. "What a freaking commotion."

The Chief chose that moment to come along the corridor. "Inspector, what is all that noise about? Please come with me."

The twins watched with an evil glint in their eyes as Shona was led off. She, on the other hand, was thinking of lambs and slaughter.

"What is going on, Shona? Why are that pair in my station again?"

"Because they're up to their thick Slavic necks in dirty deeds as usual, Sir."

"Do you have any proof of this? You seem to be singularly lacking in proof any time you arrest them. They appear to be nothing more than businessmen."

"You know they're thugs, Sir."

"Alleged thugs. Why have you got them here?"

"Because they've been bankrolling Xavier Lovelady and Pink Play Productions."

"Forgive me if I'm out of date. To my knowledge supporting the arts is not a crime."

Shona shifted in her chair. She sat on her hands. They had a sudden urge to wrap themselves around the Chief's neck.

"I wasn't implying that. I think they're money

laundering."

"You cannot go throwing accusations like that around. Do not say that to them or even hint at it. I mean it, Inspector."

"Yes, Sir." She thought fondly of how she could get his dead body on a plane to Tibet. That way she wouldn't even have to go to the funeral.

Gregor was the first man up. He was also the least bright of the twins. Shona got the impression that Stephan was the brains and Gregor the muscle. How the thugs had ended up in Dundee Shona had never managed to figure out. The pair held the Dundee crime scene in their grip. So far no one had been able to prove it. Slippery as jellied eels they managed to wriggle out of any charge ever brought against them. Witnesses bailed the minute they heard the twins were involved.

"Gregor, thank you for coming in. I need to ask you a few questions. Is that all right?"

The man looked like a startled stag - all pent up power but not knowing what way to turn. Shona being nice threw him for a loop. He stared in silence for several seconds then said, "Of course. You can ask me."

"I believe you have invested in Pink Play Productions. Is that correct?"

"I not know this information. My brother, he deal with this."

Shona was beginning to regret her choice of twin. The brighter one might have been a wiser choice. She opted for perseverance.

"Do you know anyone by the name of Jedediah Ramsbottom?"

"I do not know him."

"What about Martin Crook-Statham?"

"I know Martin."

"Do you know he's dead?"

"This I not know, but death is fact of life."

"Murder isn't."

Gregor started the roaring again. "You say I murder him. I kill you." He shot from his chair like a rocket going into orbit. Before he'd taken a couple of steps he was wrestled to the ground and then flung back into his seat. Shona had taken a couple of coppers with her. The pair of them lifted weights and looked like bulldogs. They were built for the gig of bodyguard.

"Sit still. Move one finger in my direction and I'm arresting you."

Gregor crossed his arms. With hooded eyes and puffed out chest he had the look of a vulture in full attack mode.

"Where were you on the night of...?" She rattled off the date and time.

"I was with woman. Always with woman."

"Name."

"I do not know. It is of no matter."

"It'll matter to you if you don't produce her as an alibi."

"I will find."

Shona had no doubts that a woman would be found and would trot out the relevant alibi.

"We'll be checking that out. Now, Gregor Alexeyev, I am arresting you for issuing threats..." She read him his rights and listened to his bellows as her bodyguards dragged him off.

Stephan was kept waiting whilst she slugged down a lukewarm mug of coffee. She prayed hard it would turn into a glass of Talisker whisky but to no avail. The good Lord decided that coffee would suffice. Just to be sure she poured another one and it rapidly joined its mate. Wired fit to electrocute was the only way to cope with Evil 1 and Evil 2.

As always with the twins, she got a feeling of déjà vu. They were identical in every aspect including the bellowing. The only way they could tell the difference was Gregor's intelligence levels and their fingerprints. Given her last interview she was pretty sure they'd got the right man.

"Why have you arrested my brother?" His eyes, in direct contrast to his obscenity-laden mouth, were filled with enough ice to freeze hell.

"Shut it and quit with the expletives. All I wanted to do was chat to the pair of you and now I've had a bellyful. Cooperate and you'll be out of here in half an hour."

"I will not cooperate with my persecutors."

"Why do you turn everything into a fight? I'm not persecuting you. I'm asking a few questions."

"I will not answer."

"Then you'll be experiencing the hospitality of Her Majesty in one of our cells."

"You are threatening me."

Shona took several deep breaths and held onto the edge of the table until her knuckles were white.

"For Pete's sake, answer my freaking questions. Do you want a lawyer?" Another prayer that it would be a no. She couldn't cope with Angus Runcie as well as a brace of thuggish Russians and a Glasgow con merchant. Not without copious amounts of caffeine inside her. She was beginning to wish she'd had three mugs. *I wonder if I could get away with nipping out for another one. I might take up smoking as well.*

"I do not want lawyer. I have done nothing."

Same old. Same old. They're all a bunch of ballerinas.

"What do you know about a man called Jedediah

Ramsbottom, also known as Martin Crook-Statham?"

"Nothing. I do not know this man."

"He's an actor in a movie you seem to be funding."

"I not know the actors. Is merely a business arrangement." His look dared her to say otherwise.

"What about Xavier Lovelady?"

"He is an acquaintance."

"For an acquaintance you seem to have dug him out of some gargantuan holes."

"What is the meaning of gargat..?"

"Gargantuan. Means huge. A lot like the amount of money you've got stashed away. So why did you dig him out of bankruptcy?"

"A business arrangement is all. I did favour for friend."

"Where were you on the night of…"

"With my wife."

Shona's jaw dropped so far and fast it nearly parted company with her face. When did Evil 1 get married? She'd missed that little tidbit.

"We'll be checking that out. You're free to go."

"My brother will be free also."

"Not on your nelly. He's staying here until I sort his charges out."

That was a cue for another charge at her. The policeman grabbed him. Stephan broke from his captors and took a swing at Shona. Jason, who'd stayed in the interview room with her, pushed her out of the way. Stephan's meaty fist landed square on Jason's nose. He yelped and grabbed it. Bright red blood spread through his fingers and dripped onto his blue shirt.

"Stephan Alexeyev I am arresting you for assaulting and hindering the police."

Stephan was hauled screeching out of the door and off to a cell. At least he wouldn't be leaving his brother behind.

Shona handed Jason a bunch of tissues from a box. "See if someone from uniform will give you a lift up to A&E. Are you still going out with that nurse up there?"

"Ymmph."

Shona took this to be a yes. At least he'd get to see his girlfriend.

24

There's no rest for the wicked as the saying goes, and Shona was beginning to think she had been really wicked. She still had the Buddhist monk to interview. Again. While she was busy entertaining Russia's answer to the Kray Twins, she'd set Roy on a deep dark search. Well more superficial. She wanted to know if Harry really was a Buddhist monk and if he'd changed his name by deed poll.

"The answer's yes to both, Ma'am."

"You mean he's genuine? My flabber is well and truly gasted."

"My flabber was much the same way."

"How come you didn't come up with this in the first place? You'd have saved us a lot of time."

"None of it's on the net. I had to make some phone calls."

"Be a bit more thorough next time. I can't believe the bloke's genuine."

"In all fairness, he might still be dodgy. Just changed his persona to do it."

"Good point, well put. Thanks, Roy."

"Looks like you are a monk after all, Harry."

"My name's Hui Chao. I used my Thai grandfather's name."

"Okay." She leaned forward and said in a low tone. "We need your help here. I really need to know what was said in those chats you had."

"I want to help you but I can't. The information on that recorder is confidential."

"Why for heaven's sake? There's a warrant on its

way so save us time and hand it over now."

"The recordings are for my counselling course. They're for my supervisor."

"You were speaking to them in a pub. It's not exactly Harley Street."

There was a knock at the door and Brian Gevers walked in. "Fresh from the Sheriff's office, Ma'am." He handed Shona an envelope.

"You're a top man, Brian."

She ripped the envelope open and slapped its contents down on the table.

"Hand over the recorder."

Hui Chao gazed at the paper as though it would up and do tricks. Then he ferreted around inside his voluminous robe and pulled out the recorder. "Here. You won't delete it will you?"

"No. But we might keep it as evidence. You can go now."

"How am I meant to get home?"

"You only live about ten minutes away. Surely a monk who has forgone the pleasures of this earthly life can walk in to town? Get those sandals slapping on the concrete."

"You're quite a rude woman."

"Thanks for the compliment."

When Shona returned to her office she was faced with her worst nightmare. In her absence Angus Runcie made himself comfortable in her office.

"I wondered how long it would take you to get here."

"I want the tapes of my client's interviews."

"I thought your sister dealt with one of them?"

"She's taken her daughter swimming. I'm standing in."

"Shona wasn't sure which blew her mind the most.

The fact that McCluskey had a daughter or the thought of the battleship in a swimsuit. Neither was palatable.

"The tapes please."

"Follow me."

She left Runcie in one of the interview rooms. She even offered him a coffee which he declined.

"You'd poison it."

The man had a point.

25

Once she had her office to herself Shona pulled out a packet of digestive biscuits. She downed four in quick succession. Then she headed to the kitchen to find some Arabica blend to wash them down.

She was in the midst of pouring a nice fresh brew when her phone rang.

"Drat." She grabbed the half mug and dashed back to her office.

Pressing answer on the phone she said, "DI McKenzie." She put the mug down on the table. "Oh blast."

"Shona, that's no way to speak to an eminent pathologist such as myself."

"Sorry Mary. Just managed to spill coffee everywhere. Let me grab some tissues."

A handful of tissues and a quick wipe round and she was back.

"Sorted. What can I do for you, Mary?"

"It's more, what can I do for you? I've got some results back."

"Fire away." Shona cradled the phone between her ear and shoulder, snatched a pen from the holder and pulled forward a notepad.

"I've been thinking about Jedediah Martin. Looks like he was high as a kite on cocaine. I'm wondering if it was autoerotic asphyxia by hanging?"

"In English, Mary?"

"It could have been a sex game gone wrong. High on drugs and high jinks."

"Bit of a strange place for it but I'm ruling nothing

out. Have you got anything on the skeleton in the woods?"

"A female aged about forty-five. The poor woman is still lying in my morgue. Battered over the head if the skull fractures are anything to go by. I got a few strands of hair. Brunette. Not dyed."

"Poor woman indeed. I'll get the team to search for missing women of the right age. You're a toff my dear."

"And you kissed the Blarney Stone."

Shona's head was spinning with all the strands of this investigation. She called everyone to the briefing room.

"We need an overview. Nina, present what we've got so far."

Nina did a credible job summing it up in a few succinct paragraphs.

Jason returned from Ninewells Hospital just as she finished. He was sporting a couple of black eyes and his nose glowed like Rudolph himself.

"Is it broken? Are you okay?"

"Nah, just bruising. I'm fine. I had worse than this when I was drunk after a night on the razz in the Army."

"Are you fit to report back about our woman on the hilltop?"

"There's nothing wrong with him. The lazy little sod will try to weasel his way out of work if you let him."

"Roy, back off. Jason. The corpse?"

"She belongs to the lot down at the film set. Her name's Della Fantine. Make up artist to the stars."

"I wouldnae exactly call that lot down there stars. Except Felix of course."

"Me neither. Did you manage to question anyone?"

"We did that, Ma'am."

"The scuttlebutt is that Della was madly in love with Martin. Slavered over him every chance she got."

"Mmm. Martin's peccadillos seem to be at the root of what's going on here."

"Are you thinking these are crimes of passion?" Abigail had been remarkably quiet up until then.

"Not exactly. They seem a bit too calculated for that. They weren't done in the heat of a passionate rage that's for sure. Jealousy could come into it though."

"So we're back to Sarah Martrand?"

"We are and we aren't. I think she has something to do with it but she's too slight to have done away with Martin. Also she's a bit of a wet fish. I don't think she'd have the strength to carry Della up the hill."

"If it was an autoerotic sex game gone wrong then it would be possible for her to kill Martin. She's the most likely suspect from that angle," said Abigail.

"How come everyone knows about this sex hanging thing except me?"

"There was a spate of it when I was with Highlands and Islands. No one died though."

"I thought the Highlands and Islands were quiet. Sarah had an alibi for that time though."

"What about her brother?"

"That, Jason, is a very good question." She yawned and stretched. "One we will look at tomorrow. We've all done a sixteen hour shift. Time for cocoa and pyjamas methinks."

"Time for tea. I'm starving. A man cannae live like this."

Shona, who knew he'd nipped down the canteen earlier, ignored him. She didn't care anyway as she was halfway to the door. There was a couple of large Taliskers calling her name. As were her PJs. She wondered briefly if Shakespeare had come out of her huff.

Through the door of her flat she threw her keys on the hall table and kicked off her sandals. Her feet sank into the soft carpet. Shakespeare was crying that she wanted salmon dinner. Shona obliged, opened a tin and spooned most of it into the cat's bowl. She pulled an antique crystal whisky glass from the antique cherry wood sideboard and poured a large measure of Talisker. Then she added a slug more for good measure. Curling up on the sofa she picked up the phone and dialled her parents' number. As her mother's chatter soothed her, and the cat curled up on her lap, she started to unwind. The tension of the day fell away.

26

For once she woke at a reasonable hour with no dead bodies calling for her attention. Other than the three they already had. Taking in the beautiful clear blue skies and glorious day she decided to run to work. The sun had not yet heated the air and there was just enough chill to stop overheating. A perfect running day in fact. Her long legs ate up the miles as she set a steady pace. Still arriving before anyone else she showered and tied up her hair. She donned the sea green dress she kept in her office. In her line of work clothes often got stains on them. The sort of stains most people don't mention. She was ferreting around in a cupboard looking for her spare shoes when she saw a pair of orange stilettos walk in to the room. They were adorning Nina's feet.

"Praying to Allah are we, Ma'am?"

"I'm praying to the saint of missing shoes that I find mine."

"We're the same size. You can borrow a pair of mine."

"I'd rather go barefooted. I'd break my ankle walking on those." With a triumphant look in her eyes she pulled her footwear from the depths of the cupboard. "They were lost and now they are found."

"You're awfully biblical today, Shona."

"What brings you to my office? Apart from hassling me that is."

"I've sent Roy and Jason to bring Shane Martrand in. Would you like me to interview him?"

"Please do. Push every button he's got. Then find a few more to push."

Nina departed with a crash of the door. The word

quiet didn't exist in Nina's vocabulary.

Picking up the phone, Shona dialled Della Fantine's next of kin. They'd tried to get hold of the woman the day before but not a soul was available. Still no answer. She redialled the number for the local cops in Bedfordshire.

"Detective Inspector Shona McKenzie here from Police Scotland."

"What can we do for you, Ma'am?"

"May I speak to my oppo in CID?"

"I'll see if he's in."

She listened to some piped music. Bizarrely it seemed to be a brass band playing Second World War tunes.

"Eric Slater here. How can I help you?"

"I need a couple of things." She outlined her case and explained she needed to inform Della's next of kin of her death. She also asked if they could do a search on the girl and let her know if anything turned up.

"Give me a couple of hours. You'll have everything you need."

He hung up without so much as a goodbye. A man of few words, Shona was hoping this meant he was big on action.

Roy had returned from his trip to collect Shane. He was currently occupied devouring a doughnut and drinking a large can of Irn-Bru, Scotland's other national drink.

"I'm glad to see that this new adult side of you is embracing healthy eating. Doughnuts for breakfast are not exactly nutritious."

"It's a fine breakfast, Ma'am. I need the energy. I'm sure you'll have me working hard enough to burn it all off."

"I'd be more worried about diabetes than putting

on weight if I were you. With what you're eating you'll have more energy than you'll ever want or need. Bananas give you energy as well."

"A banana? Are you trying to kill me? You're worse than my mum."

"Much as I'd love to discuss the state of your diet, there's work to be done. What was the deal with Xavier's finances?"

"Up to his pretty little thespian ears in debt. Looks like even the Kalashnikov twins weren't keen on bailing him out this time."

"That's interesting. They're usually keen to make a killing. In more ways than one. What level of debt are we talking about?"

"Roughly a million and a half. Maybe a bit more, maybe a bit less."

"Dollars or pounds?"

"Pounds. He knows how to do it in style does Xavier."

"I wonder if Pa Broon knows about all of this. I might have a chat with him. If he's funding the operation and it's in debt he won't be best pleased."

"Yep. The ex Lord Provost is all about making oodles of cash. Cash going down the drain wouldn't fit in with his plans at all."

She yelled over to Abigail. "Can you ask Pa Broon to come in for a chat? Let him know it's to his advantage."

She turned back to Roy. "I've another little job for you."

"Your wish is my command."

"Cheeky blighter. Get Harry's Dictaphone out of evidence. Listen to every conversation on it. Prepare handouts for the team on its contents."

Roy saluted, stood up and headed in the direction of the evidence room.

Shona headed in the direction of a cup of coffee. She didn't make it that far.

27

The Chief's secretary accosted her in the corridor. "The boss wants to see you."

"Am I in bother?"

"You're always in bother." The secretary grinned. "He didn't seem that upset so I think you're fine."

The Chief barely looked up as she walked in.

"Sir?"

"Release the Alexeyevs without charge."

"What? They're as guilty as all get out. One of them threatened me and the other one punched PC Roberts. We've got it all on video."

"Yes we do and I have looked at that video."

"So why are we letting them off scot-free?"

"Because, Inspector, you deliberately antagonised them. I have warned you repeatedly to keep your temper in rein."

"I did no such thing."

"Yes you did. It has come back to haunt you. Maybe it will make you think in future."

Shona couldn't move. She couldn't take it in.

"That will be all, Inspector."

Shona left the room wondering if she could hire Gregor to kill the Chief. Then she could get rid of him and lock Gregor up. Score.

"You want me to do what?" The look on Peter's face said it all.

"You heard me correctly. Boot the Ruskies out on to the street. All charges to be dropped."

"Are we ever going to bring the pair of them to justice?"

"I doubt it, Abigail. I very much doubt it."

"I think I'll ring the Triads and see if they can help us out. They might make them disappear from the face of the earth."

"That's as good a plan as any. Can the pair of you do a search on HOLMES? Missing women aged about forty-five and roughly five foot four in height. Likely a brunette."

They both groaned but turned to their computers.

Pa Broon arrived at the station meek as a lamb. He held out his hand and shook Shona's. "How nice to see you. You believe I have something that can help you?"

Shona had a sudden urge to use gel spray to clean her hand.

"Lord Provost. Thank you for coming. My office is a little small so I hope you don't mind using an interview room."

The smooth guy act disappeared. "Am I being interviewed in regards to a case?"

"Not at all, Sir. We have information which we think will be advantageous to you."

They sat down. "I need to switch the recording equipment on but you are not being interviewed. This is merely a chat."

He nodded.

"For the benefit of the recording this is not an interview. Lord Provost Brown is aware that he is not having his rights read to him and has agreed. He is also aware that anything said in this room is confidential."

Pa Broon nodded.

"I believe you have invested money in the movie currently being filmed by Pink Play Productions?"

"Yes, I do. That's not a crime." A wary look appeared in Brown's eyes.

"Absolutely. We are not accusing you of a crime.

Are you aware that Xavier Lovelady has a large amount of debt?"

"Impossible. How much is this so-called debt?" He leaned back in his chair and gazed at her with a look of utter boredom.

"Over a million pounds."

The boredom soon passed as he shot upright.

"What, you mean he's been playing fast and loose with my money?"

"It certainly seems that way. Now we will do everything to ensure your money is safe." Shona felt physically sick trying to be nice to the man. "However, we are going to need your help."

"I'll help by killing him."

"Please, Lord Provost. This is not the place to be issuing threats."

Please kill him. I can lock you up and never have to deal with you again.

"You're right. What can I do to help?"

"I need you to keep me informed of any conversations you have with him. Please do not bring this up directly. If you do, you'll be saying goodbye to your investment."

"You can count on me." The large man stood up, shook her hand once more, and left.

Shona switched off the recording equipment and went to wash her hands. She scrubbed them long and hard. Still, like Lady Macbeth, she felt unclean.

"I've been a cop in this city since I was eighteen. I never thought I'd see a day when George Broon would be helping us with oor enquiries. I mean genuinely helping. No' the type where we're investigating him."

"It came as much of a shock to me, Peter."

"We got our crooks to help us all the time in Highlands and Islands."

"Thanks for your input. Truly helpful, Abigail. Not!"

"Well, you know, it worked for us. Saying that, it was mainly poachers dobbing in other petty crooks. They kept an eye out for us. We turned a blind eye to the odd rabbit or salmon."

"Did they keep your larder stocked as well?"

Abigail's grin lit up her face. "Funny you should say that."

"I seriously don't want to know any more."

"I make a mean hare stew. My mum can do wonders with venison in Scottish Chinese fusion cooking."

"Be sure to bring some back next time you visit. In the meantime we've a couple of murder enquiries to run."

"How did the interview with Shane go?"

"The man's a brute. Thick as a mealy pudding."

"We can't arrest someone for being thick."

"Good job as you'd have to arrest Soldier Boy," said Roy.

"If you had two brain cells they'd refuse to speak to each other."

"Boys that's enough. I thought this rivalry was over. I don't want it rearing its ugly head."

"We're jesting, Ma'am. No need to get worried."

"Jest about something else. Like how you're going to work together to solve this crime."

They looked at each other and laughed. "You don't ask for much do you?"

Ignoring them, Shona said, "Shane? Let's focus."

"By trade he's a gravedigger. The muscles on his arms would give Popeye's mate a run for his money."

"You mean Bluto? He was Popeye's enemy."

"I didn't have you down as a comic fan, Peter. We don't need a lesson in the finer points of Popeye the

Sailor man. Not today."

"Whatever. His muscles are huge. His thighs are quite strong as well."

"So you're saying he'd have the strength to have done our murders?"

"Definitely. I'm not sure he'd have the brains though."

"You don't need many brains to kill someone and dump them on a hill," said Roy. "Just brute force."

"True." Shona was willing to let them think through all the angles.

"You might need a few more brains to work out how to hang them," Jason chipped in.

"Or access to a computer and google," said Nina.

"So Martrand had the means and the motive to kill. Alibis?"

"No alibi for Martin. Went to the pub with his sister and then went home alone. Tucked up with his teddy bear and his thumb in his mouth by midnight."

"Nina, don't be so irreverent. What about an alibi for Della's murder?"

"Said he was out walking as he couldn't sleep. Too worried about his sister."

"Let me think about it. I need to make a couple of phone calls and I'll be back. I'll speak to Douglas to see if we have enough for an arrest."

"Mind and be nice to him now, Ma'am. We dinnae want him being upset."

Shona threw a pen in his general direction and left them to it.

28

Before she managed to ring the Procurator Fiscal for advice her phone rang.

"Shona, it's Eric Slater from Bedfordshire. I've got that info you wanted."

"Good stuff."

"The reason you couldn't get hold of Della's next of kin is because she's dead."

"Crumbs. When?"

"That's the saddest part. We didn't get an answer at the door. A neighbour popped out to see us and said she hadn't been seen in months. She was a bit worried. We smashed the door down and the poor woman was dead in the kitchen. Been there about three months they reckon."

"How awful. I take it Della and her mother…" She paused and thought. "Is it her mother?"

"Foster mother. The neighbour said she hadn't seen Della around for about nine months."

"Possibly estranged then. Any other next of kin?"

"Della's foster grandfather is in care. Alzheimer's."

"What a sad family. Did anything come up about Della?"

"Yes. She's known to us. A couple of years ago she was stalking some poor bloke who was married with two kids. She said he was in love with her. He said they'd only ever said hello in passing. In the end, there was a restraining order taken out against her."

"Sounds like a right nut."

"She really was according to my colleagues. Kept on and was arrested a couple of times. Got off with a warning, as she wasn't dangerous, just obsessed. Then it just stopped and she disappeared."

Shona said her goodbyes and hung up.

A police diver interrupted her in the act of ringing Douglas.

"Morning, Ma'am. A little pressie for you." He handed over a huge evidence bag. Inside was a baseball bat. "This might be what you're looking for. You don't find many of those in the River Tay. We did find two prams and a motorbike though. Waste of a good bike. They could have sent it to a scrap merchants if it was knackered. No need to go cluttering up a river with it."

"You're a star. I could kiss you."

The lad laughed. "Nah, you're all right. The PF's pals with my dad. He'd kill me if I started snogging his girlfriend."

Shona couldn't help but join in. She phoned through to the briefing room and asked Iain to come to her office. She handed him the evidence bag. "Check this for blood. If it's a match for Martin then we have our weapon. See if you can get prints from it as well."

"You don't ask for much, Ma'am. It's been in a cold river for a few days so there might be nothing to find. I'll see what I can do."

"Do your best." She was speaking to his rapidly disappearing back. Iain loved his job. So much so he'd rather be dabbling about in chemicals in his lair than speaking to real live human beings.

She finally managed to ring Douglas to find he was in a meeting. "He'll be out in about ten minutes. Ring back then, Shona."

"Thanks, Carol. Tell him not to budge. It's official business this time."

She popped into the briefing room and gave the team a fifteen-minute break. "That's fifteen real minutes, not fifteen Roy minutes." Roy's attitude had improved a hundred-fold. His timekeeping had deteriorated in direct proportion.

29

It was nearer half an hour before she could speak to Douglas. His professional advice was to hang fire for now.

"Your evidence is solid but blood and fingerprint evidence would make it watertight."

"I thought you might say that."

"You don't want the case to fall through the cracks because you haven't been thorough."

"You're right. In the meantime, I'm going to check if anyone else has upset Della. I'm going to ask Uniform for some protection for them."

"Sounds like a plan." His voice dropped a couple of octaves. It set Shona's brain into overdrive and sent shivers down her spine. "Am I going to see you tonight?"

"Definitely. Well, as definite as I can be with a case on."

"We can tuck Alice into bed early. Rory's got a new computer game so he'll be in his room. There's an expensive bottle of merlot with our name on it."

"It's a date." Shona found her own voice had gone husky.

"We've managed a whole conversation and not a dead body in sight."

"Bye, Douglas." She hung up as waves of heat swept through her body. "Roll on tonight. How am I meant to concentrate?"

She found her computer and every other inanimate object in the room wasn't interested.

"Hang fire until the forensics are back on the baseball bat."

"What baseball bat? First I've heard of it," said Nina.

"Whoops. Forgot that momentous piece of information hadn't been relayed. Sorry. The divers came up with a baseball bat. Iain's checking it out as we speak."

"Your wee chat with the PF got you all flustered has it?"

"Beautifully put, Peter. It also happens to be true. However, you'd be better focusing on your work than my love life."

"What do you want us to do?" said Jason. "We're a bit stalled at the moment."

"Find out if anyone else has upset Sarah. We need to ask Uniform to keep a bit of an eye on them. Think up some excuse for a bunch of coppers to be milling around at the film set."

"They could pretend they're star-struck." said Abigail.

"They wouldn't need to pretend. Some of the women down there are fit as well. I wouldn't mind dating them."

"Felix is pretty easy on the eye as well," added Nina.

"Calm down the lot of you. Felix is out of bounds. He's married to minor royalty. The rest of them are out of bounds because … Well just because I say so. Leave well alone."

"Peter and Abigail. Look into the possible whereabouts of Mr Zhou. I'm aware we've done nothing to investigate his disappearance. Abigail you can head that one up as you speak Cantonese. You'll be able to communicate more easily."

"Do you want me to ring the Hong Kong police as well, Ma'am?"

"Yes. See what you can find out. I also want a list

of all those missing women on my desk."

The team scurried to do her bidding. They might be stalled in one area but there was still plenty to be done.

Shona popped down to Mary's office.

"You here again? Much as it's nice to see you, I've not got anything on your latest body as yet. Not that you don't already know anyway."

"It's not that. I was wondering if you knew what sort of weapon was used to bludgeon our skeleton to death? Could it have been a baseball bat?"

"I'd have to look into that in greater detail. Can't give an answer right now. Why do you ask?"

She explained about the weapon found in the Tay.

"It's never dull with you around, Shona. Leave it with me and I'll get back to you."

"Thanks, Mary. If you could do it—"

"Soonest. I know the drill." her wry smile took the sting from her words.

.

30

The list with the names of the missing women was on her desk when she returned. Shona picked it up. Four names, all of which had been chosen with love and hope by their parents over forty years ago. That hope changed in an instant when, during a Dundee winter, each of them disappeared. An icy hand grabbed her stomach and squeezed. Could their disappearance be related? Not to this case but an entirely different case altogether. Bile rose in her throat. She fired up HOLMES and checked the dates when they went missing.

Meredith Crayford - January 2016
Yvonne Bear - February 2016
Morag McAllister - December 2015
Leanna Smith - January 2016

She added the details to the list of names then dialled the first number. One by one she went about dispensing hope and fear in a few sentences. Nothing but a bundle of consonants, vowels and syllables. Yet together they had the power to break people's hearts. Ten minutes was all it took. Each of the relatives she spoke to agreed to bring in a personal item to be used for DNA. Shona leaned back in her chair and closed her eyes. She loved her job but sometimes the sheer sadness of the things she had to do overwhelmed her. Responsibilities weighed heavily.

"It would appear nearly everyone in the company's upset Sarah at some point. She was a sensitive soul," said Peter.

"What they actually said was, 'She was a big girl's blouse. She'd get upset at the sight of a paper bag blowing in the wind'," said Roy.

"One quote, 'You only had to look at her sideways and she'd weep. Then she'd go running to that infernal brother of hers'," added Abigail.

"Great, so the whole cast need protecting. Are there coppers swarming about the place?"

"Not yet. Uniform say that they're busy. Can't spare the manpower."

"What was really said was, 'Tell Shona McKenzie to use her own manpower. It's costing me a fortune to keep her in officers.'"

"Damn. I'll ask the Chief to fund it. He's trying to keep Louis Starkind sweet so he'll probably dig deep."

She left to do it straight away. All joking apart they needed to keep the crew safe and out of harm's way. At least they were all in one small space so easier to protect.

The Chief sounded weary. "How long for, Shona?"

"Today at least, a couple of days at most. Then we'll have made an arrest."

He pulled a pad out of his drawer, filled in a few details, tore off the sheet and pushed it across the table.

"Your get out of jail free card."

"Thank you. Sir. I appreciate it."

"You mean he coughed it up as sweet as?" Roy put the incredulous feeling of every team member into words.

"Yep. Sweeter in fact."

"Ma'am, I thought you'd be arguin' until tea time."

"Me too, but there we have it. Louis Starkind and European royalty have got the Chief tamed."

"Have we got anything on our Mr Zhou yet, Abigail?"

"Nothing. He was a well respected businessman. No money troubles. No arguments or disputes with anyone else. He was a fair man and popular with his staff and colleagues."

"Is it possible for everyone to be that nice all the time?"

"If he had enemies, as Chinese we would know about it. These things are talked about widely."

"Family life?"

"Married with two sons and Miriam, his only daughter."

"What do they do?"

"The sons work in the family business. Miriam is here to study English before starting a PhD in International Economics."

Shona leaned her chin on her steepled hands. "Doesn't sound like any of them would want to bump him off. Do you think the sons might have bumped him off to get their hands on the family riches earlier?"

"I'll look into it." She jotted down a note and sat back.

Nina stopped suddenly and stared into space.

"'You all right, Nina?" said Shona. 'You look like you're having an absence seizure."

"I'm good. Just had an idea. Wasn't Mr Zhou one of the investors in Pink Play Productions? I wonder if he had anything to do with Sarah Martrand?"

"Good point, Nina. Look into it. Abigail find out why he invested in such a tinpot outfit in Dundee. With his billions you'd think he'd prefer to invest in a huge Hollywood movie."

"Do you think he might have dealings wi' Shane

Martrand as well?"

"Find out, Peter. You lot get on with it and see what you can find. Roy, come to my office."

31

Roy and Shona grabbed drinks en route. Shona pulled out a packet of chocolate digestives. They munched in companionable silence for a few minutes.

Shona wiped her mouth and said, "Bring me up to speed on the results of the Dictaphone analysis."

"Mostly just people chatting. They do tend to bare their souls to him. Most of it the 'no one understands me or recognises my talent' kind. The usual guff lovey's seem to trot out."

"That's not exactly PC, Roy, but we'll let it go this once." *Mainly because I agree with him.* "Anything else thrown up?"

"Sonya Chey is pregnant. She's not sure if the baby is Martin's or his father, Louis's."

"What? Are you for real? Who the devil is Sonya Chey? I can't recall her."

"American actress. Hails from the Bronx. Plays Kathleen Scott the wife of our esteemed Captain."

"So you're telling me she was sleeping with father and son?"

"Give the lady a cuddly toy. It gets more interesting though." He handed over a sheet of paper.

"It would seem that Martin hated the woman. He thought the part should be played by a Brit," said Shona.

"Yep. He was using her for bonking whenever he felt like it."

"Roy. Please use more genteel speech."

"I'm a male copper. I'm not going to be speaking like a wee girlie."

"No but you could moderate it slightly when I'm

144

around."

"So someone else for our Sarah, and consequently Shane, to hate. Any other intrigue?" She glanced down at the paper.

Roy let her read it in peace and then said, "Someone was blackmailing Xavier and Martin."

"Bullseye." Roy threw an imaginary dart.

"That's a reason to kill, not get killed."

"Maybe Martin was refusing to pay out. Might have been teaching him a lesson."

"I agree. Also it puts out a message that anyone declining the offer would be offed as well."

"They're a right hotbed of intrigue and scandal that wee company."

"Beautifully put, Roy. Never a truer word. Let's go. We're going to go and have a word with Xavier and Sonya."

"They won't be happy that you've stopped filming."

"Do I look like I care?"

She grabbed her handbag and they left for Riverside.

The sun bouncing off the river provided a stunning vista. Shona took a slight detour so they drove down Riverside and could take in the full beauty of the scene.

"Dundee's not half a bonnie place to live."

"I know. We tend to forget that when we're busy digging up bodies and dealing with lowlifes."

The filming was in full swing, all technical difficulties having been resolved. They stood and watched for a little while. Felix Fotheringham-Farington was stunning in his portrayal of Scott.

"He's good, Ma'am."

"He is that. This lot are more professional than I give them credit for. I can almost believe I'm getting ready to go to the Antarctic."

"They must be sweating cobs under all those clothes. Dundee normally feels like the Antarctic but it's about a hundred degrees in the shade."

"They've picked the wrong time for sure. I suppose they're lucky it's not raining."

"I don't like to interrupt filming."

"No need. The dead bodies are not going anywhere. Let's watch until there's a natural break. We might as well enjoy ourselves."

32

After an hour Shona regretted her words. She'd obviously jinxed the investigation.

"If they're not here where are they? Where can we find them?"

"Sonya Chey's nowhere to be seen. She's meant to be here filming a tearful farewell as I leave for my voyage. Should be quite moving."

"Have you looked for her?"

"My dear lady, of course." His brilliant smile had Shona forgetting her hatred of the moniker 'dear lady'. It also had her forgetting the Procurator Fiscal.

"Where?"

"Sent someone to her hotel room. No answer. Tried her mobile. Same result. She's probably up in orbit dancing with the stars. She's a user."

"Uses what?"

"Legal prescription drugs mainly. Nothing off the street as far as I know."

"And this doesn't bother you from a professional point of view?"

"Darling, we'd have no one left to act in any movies if it did."

"Is that for real?"

"Of course not, darling. It's a gross exaggeration. It does happen more often than you think though."

"Excuse me for a minute. Don't go away."

She moved to a quiet area and pulled out her phone. "Jason get yourself down to where the actors are staying. Find out if Sonya Chey is around." She listened. "Ring me when you've been."

"I've got my boys out looking for her." She looked

around. "Where's Xavier?"

"He's been sacked."

"Sacked?"

Felix took in the gormless look on her face. "Happens all the time my dear. In this case the investors didn't like all the bad publicity. Critics are beginning to liken our film to The Scottish Play."

"They think it's cursed?"

"They do. And they think Xavier is the one that's cursing it."

"Any idea where he is?"

"None whatsoever. He stormed off and no one's seen him at the hotel."

"Who's producing the movie now?"

"I'm standing in temporarily. Clarissa Claris-Beauchamp is expected any day."

"Who's she?"

"Highly acclaimed producer. Former child actress. Gave up acting at eighteen. Changed tack to producing. Jolly successful at it too. I need to get back to the movie now. Delays cost money."

"I'm sure that's true. If I delay it costs lives. I think I'm top trumps."

His brown eyes changed from twinkling to a lightning flash of evil. "I wasn't aware this was a competition."

He was right. Shona looked contrite "I agree, but I need to catch this killer or you might not have any cast to direct. I'll be in touch if there's anything to report."

"I'm sure Xavier is accounted for somewhere. My gut tells me that Sonya's absence does not bode well," said Shona.

"My gut's saying exactly the same thing. Best case scenario she's nursing a hangover. Next best scenario she's unconscious due to a drugs overdose."

"I don't even want to think about worst case scenario."

"Ma'am, with you involved that's probably the most likely."

"That's what I'm worried about."

They climbed into the pool car she'd borrowed and she switched on the ignition.

33

The imposing figure strolled into the hotel, confidence oozing from every pore. This was someone who was expected to be here. Who took command of the area and filled it with a presence that filled the space and exuded an aura of gravitas and power. And yet, rather than standing out, this allowed them to blend into the background. Another businessman on his way to a meeting. The hotel saw many of these. All of whom thought they were the most important person there. They were the most important person alive.

They strode through the modern, glass-filled lobby and over to the lift. It was activated with a pre-arranged keycard. They walked along the corridor, barely noticing the numbers on the doors. Arriving at the correct door the keycard was slapped against the contact. A quick push of the handle and the door opened. An uninvited guest who would come to the party anyway.

Inside it was dark. The figure strode to the window and opened the curtains. Light flooded in chasing away every dark shadow. A woman lay on the bed. Her voluptuous breasts strained at a black and red negligée. Red hair, long and thick, formed a pool around her head. The sunlight picked out the copper hues. She murmured in her sleep and shifted slightly.

The room stank of booze as the figure moved to the bed. They picked up the woman's arm and squeezed tightly. The woman groaned but barely moved. The figure had seen to this the previous night. A mixture of cocktails and tablets and the woman was out for the count. The uninvited guest pulled out a pre-filled syringe from their briefcase. Thinking of the Kray Twins who had perfected this many years before, they pulled a tourniquet out as well. It was expertly applied and the syringe pushed into the bulging vein. Another groan and the arm moved slightly. It was held in a firm grip so the syringe remained. The plunger was pushed and the woman descended into heroine overdose hell. Death followed swiftly.

Checking the corridor the figure slipped from the room. The confident stance was back as they left the hotel. Long strides took them towards the city centre. Old buildings, the scars of the passing years highlighting their destitution, soon hid the figure from sight.

.

34

Shona had no sooner pointed the nose of the car in the direction of the car park exit than her phone rang. There being no 'hands free' in the clapped out vehicle she ordered Roy to answer it.

He rifled about in her handbag. "What have you got in here?"

"Just answer the damn phone."

He snatched it in the nick of time and said, "Inspector McKenzie's phone."

A tinny voice. Then, "Great. I'll let her know." He hung up.

"That great did not sound triumphal."

"It was more despondent."

"Hit me with it."

"That was Jason. Sonya Chey is dead. Looks like she's injected herself with an overdose of something as yet unknown."

Shona, for once, had no words to articulate how she was feeling. She changed direction and drove to the hotel.

When they arrived there was an ambulance at the door of the hotel. The paramedics had made an attempt to resuscitate but to no avail. They had pronounced the body dead and were waiting for her arrival. The POLSA was busy setting up the crime scene.

Shona peered through the bedroom door but couldn't see much. "Can I go in?"

The POLSA asked her if she could wait ten minutes. He wanted to make sure the crime scene was secure first. She was happy to oblige and spent the time quizzing Jason.

"What was she like when you found her?"

"She was lying on the bed looking like a ghost with a tan."

"Strange description but I get what you mean. Did you touch her?"

"Tried for a pulse in her neck. It was obvious she was past help. I got the medics in anyway."

"Good call. Did you touch anything in the room?"

"No. I did take loads of photos though." He whipped out his phone and started a slide show. "It's a high spec phone so the photos are crystal clear."

"Nice one. You did good Jason."

He grinned ear to ear. After his shenanigans with the hangover he was desperate to make a good impression. She smiled back, his transgressions forgotten.

She tried to make the images larger. From what she could see Sonya was lying at a strange angle on the bed. There was a tourniquet on her right arm and a syringe lying on the bed next to her.

"No one in there touched that did they?"

"I don't know. I've been out here since the paramedics arrived."

"Thank heavens we've got photos. That was a smart move."

She studied the images intently until she was allowed to see the real thing.

In Shona's experience deaths in hotels usually involved rooms the size of a medium sized larder. Pink Play Productions were obviously paying big bucks because Sonya's room was roughly half the size of a ballroom. The woman still had the tourniquet on. The syringe hadn't budged from the spot indicated by the photos. She was now sporting a Venflon in the other arm. She looked peaceful as though she'd drifted off to sleep.

Which is in fact what she had done. Drifted off to sleep and forgotten to breathe. Her vibrant red hair formed a halo around her head. She resembled a Pre-Raphaelite painting of a woman in repose. The bodice of her nightdress added to the illusion.

Shona turned to the paramedics who were waiting for her go ahead to leave. "What's your thoughts on what might have killed her?"

"We're not allowed to say. Has to be a doctor. I can tell you that there's heroin prep paraphernalia over there."

There was indeed a spoon, with what looked like a drop of liquid heroin on it.

"What a sad way to end your life. Alone in a hotel room, far from home."

Iain arrived and got to work taking photos. Together with Jason's photos they would provide a comprehensive overview of the crime scene. She watched him take a clos- up of the teaspoon. Upmarket, the hotel had its crest engraved on the handle. They were about to be missing a teaspoon.

"Roy, get that into evidence."

He hurried over and did as he was asked. He trotted off to give it to the POLSA.

"Do you think Whitney will come?" said Jason.

"Unlikely given that the paramedics have pronounced her."

"Shona, I leave you to your own devices and another dead body appears."

She whirled around to face him. "Douglas." The warmth in her voice brought the temperature in the air conditioned room up a couple of degrees.

"You really have to get a new hobby. Collect china cats or something. The sort of thing a normal person does."

"They do seem to appear with frightening

regularity. Trust me I'd rather be collecting cats. It's much more soothing on the nerves."

Douglas threw his head back and laughed. "Have you met Shakespeare?"

"You have a point. There must be something less stressful than body collecting."

"Try reading a library book."

"I might just do that. If I ever get time off from solving murders that is."

"What you got here?"

"Suspected overdose."

"You might want to check whether she was left or right-handed. Addicts tend to inject into their non-dominant arm using their dominant hand to insert the needle and push the plunger."

"So if it's backside foremost then someone else did the pushing?"

"Yes. That doesn't mean it's murder of course. Just that someone helped them. If it then went wrong it would be manslaughter not murder."

"I'd say in this case it probably means she was murdered if someone else was involved."

"I'd say you're right. As the Procurator Fiscal I'd say make a call of murder if it's in the wrong arm. Given the other deaths in Pink Play Productions I think we can safely say we've got ourselves a serial killer."

"I'll examine Shane Martrand's relationship with the girl. I'm sure it's not good given that she might be pregnant with Martin's baby."

"I don't doubt it. Right I'm off to a meeting. See you later." With a cheerful wave he walked off along the corridor.

After about an hour they came to cart the body off to the morgue. It had been photographed from every angle and every surface of the room examined and dusted for prints. They'd even gone through her drawer and her handbag to look for evidence. Her handbag had the usual accoutrements that any woman carts around. It also contained several bottles of prescription pills. These were bagged and taken into evidence.

"Mary will need them to match against toxicology," said Shona.

This was Shona's team's cue to leave the POLSA to the crime scene. She collected Roy from the coffee shop where he was busy buying takeaway coffee. For once she could have kissed him.

"Roy, you're a legend." She pulled the cup from his hand and took a sip of the scalding liquid. It burned all the way down but she didn't care. The caffeine hit was needed, as was the fluid.

35

Now they had four bodies and a missing mogul. Alongside that was a disgruntled producer who might or might not be missing and an unborn child. Shona explained all this to the Chief.

"Surely, Inspector, you should be able to identify a murderer within such a closed community of people?"

"You would think so, Sir. In all fairness it could be someone from outside targeting the production. Maybe a rival company?"

"Unlikely. Look into it anyway. I've got Louis Starkind giving me all sorts of grief about this production."

"Talking of Louis. I need to interview him."

"Absolutely not. The Prime Minister will be on the phone to me before he's in an interview room."

"Unavoidable I'm afraid. He could be the father of Sonya Chey's unborn baby."

His face went grey. Shona got ready to grab his GTN spray and force it into his mouth.

The Chief took in her changed stance. "I'm fine, Shona. No need to rush to the rescue."

Shona still wasn't sure. He'd already had one heart attack due to her antics on a previous case. Driving him to another one did not sit well with her.

"Will there ever be a day when you carry out an investigation without upsetting half of Britain?"

"If I interview Felix I'll be upsetting half of Europe. The royal variety as well."

"Stop being so impudent."

"Not impudent, Sir. Just stating a fact." Her voice sounded quite cheery at the prospect.

"Give me an hour to brief the Chief Constable and the Prime Minister. The PM will be made aware of the importance of confidentiality."

"Will do, Sir. I've other lines of enquiry to follow up on in the meantime."

"Off you go and follow them then."

As she walked from the room she could swear she heard him say, "Follow them all the way to the Antarctic. The real Antarctic."

That's not very nice. If I do, I'll be burying you in the Arctic tundra. This thought cheered her right up.

"What's making you so cheery, Ma'am? It's no' like you to be as happy as this in the middle of a case. Especially when it's going nowhere."

"Cases. Remember the woman in the woods."

"Oh, aye. Cases."

"Is Iain around? I need an update on the baseball bat. Also, could you chase up the items from the missing women?"

"I've not heard they're in evidence."

"Me neither. That's why we need to chase it up."

"Iain's gone down the canteen for a pile of sarnies. He'll be back before you can say DNA."

"Send him in my direction when he reappears. Oh. I nearly forgot. Get someone to ask the film crew if Sonya was right or left-handed."

Iain came bearing gifts. One was a plate of mixed sandwiches, which he placed on her desk with a flourish. The other was the DNA results form the baseball bat.

She grabbed the paperwork. Traces of blood on the bat, which were the same as Martin's. "We have a match."

"Looks like it."

"Where can you buy baseball bats in Dundee?"

"Probably a lot of places but not this one. It's used in America only. No exports to other countries."

"The only American around here is Della Fantine. The baseball bat was hers?"

"Looks very much like it, Ma'am. In fact I'd stake my pension on it."

"All we need to do now is work out who had access to it. Were there any fingerprints?"

"The wood had been in water for a couple of days. That's what took the time. I had to dry it out. The answer - it was crawling with fingerprints all overlapping. No use for evidence."

"I suppose that's inevitable given it's a baseball bat. One friendly game and that's the evidence ruined. Perfect to use as a weapon in a murder case."

"Couldn't be better."

"Our killer knows exactly what they are doing."

"Don't they always. I'm off to start analyzing what we got from the hotel room."

As Jason left, Peter walked in. "Sonya was right handed."

"So it's looking like murder."

"How do you figure that out? It's a bit of a big leap."

She outlined what Douglas had said to her.

"He's a clever chap that PF."

"He certainly is. Changing tack, have the personal effects come in for the DNA analysis?"

"They have. Logged into evidence."

"Why didn't we know about this?"

"Bertha, who runs evidence, collapsed with a bleeding ulcer. Happened while the evidence was arriving. It was logged in but no one sent the info out about it needing to be picked up."

"Get Jason or Roy to take it down to evidence."

"Aye."

"In about an hour we need to get Louis Starkind in for questioning. Can you do the interview with me?"

"That'll be fun."

"That's not the way I would have put it."

36

In the end they had to wait for a couple of hours before they could interview dear Louis. The Chief Constable of Police Scotland informed them he wanted to be in the interview. This involved a lot of 'hurry up and wait' as he was driven across from Glasgow. Especially since there was a smash on the A90 and nothing was moving. Not even the Chief Constable himself could sort it out. This left them twiddling their thumbs and watching the clock. Shona spent her time harassing Iain, asking him to hurry up with the DNA results.

"Ma'am, I'm good but I'm not God. I can't work miracles."

"Can you hurry it up at all?"

"No. With all due respect I'll get it done a heck of a lot faster if you leave me to it."

She did just that and went to hassle Roy instead. He was occupying himself by updating Facebook and Twitter.

"That better be the official pages and not your personal accounts."

"Mixture of both. Uploading to the official accounts. Sharing from my personal accounts."

"Ask Felix if he'll come in. They must be finished filming by now. The sun will be the wrong shade or something. Abigail and I will interview him. You can do another search of the web for anything on Louis Starkind."

"The web will be awash with stories about him."

"I need to find out if he's ever been violent. Keep it under your hat and report straight to me."

"I'm on it."

"Felix, thank you for coming in. I need to ask you a few more questions."

"Of course, Inspector. I'll do whatever I can to help the police."

"You were friends with Martin a long time?"

"Yes, since we were five and started boarding school together."

"So you'd say you know him well."

"Better than anyone else alive."

"I've heard talk of his father, but not his mother. Is she dead?"

"That's the story that they put out. She's actually committed long term to a mental health facility. Early onset Alzheimer's. Been there for several years."

"How awful. How did Martin feel about that?"

"He blamed his father all the way. Said that he drove her to it."

"Did he have a good relationship with his mother?"

"As good as one can have when one is away from her for much of the year."

"What about his father?"

"They hated each other. A deep hatred born of Louis's bullying."

"Are you saying Louis bullied Martin?"

"Yes. Everyone knew it. Louis thought Martin was a snivelling brat. When he grew up he said Martin was a disgrace to the profession."

"What was he like as an actor?"

"He was a truly brilliant actor. He was held back because of his father. Louis made sure no one hired him."

"Are you saying this because he was your best friend?"

"No, I'm saying it because it's true. Louis was terrified Martin would steal the limelight."

"Felix, you've been very helpful. Thank you."

He stood up, picked Shona's hand up, and kissed it. "Thank you my dear lady. Now, I must away to my wife." With this he swivelled round and walked out of the door as though he had taken on the persona of Captain Scott himself.

"Roy, dish the dirt."

"I can't find any dirt, Ma'am. In fact, it's sickening. Everyone loves Louis. Not one negative thing about him on the net. It's impossible."

"Probably because he bullied people into taking it down. Sounds like he ruled the movie industry with an iron fist."

"How come he's had so much time to be milling around in Dundee? You'd think he'd be acting out somewhere else. Hotshot Hollywood superstar like him."

"You'd think so. Just our luck he's landed here. I think he's going for the sympathy vote. He's playing the role of grieving father." Shona struck a pose to emphaise the point.

"I don't know what role he'll be playing when I interview him."

"At least you'll have the Chief Constable to back you up."

"Or crucify me. He and the Chief might be planning on throwing me to the wolves."

Whilst Shona and Roy were chatting the others had been giving the place a bit of a spruce-up. Mo's husband had died and she wouldn't be back until after the funeral. This meant the place looked like a bomb site and smelled like a sewer. Shona, too busy to take them to task for it, was grateful that Peter had them hard at it.

"Good show chaps. Better sit down and look busy now though. The big boss should be here any minute now."

Shona popped in to see Iain.

"Ma'am, it's not here yet. I've sent it over to the main lab. They'll ring you the minute it's done."

She returned to her office and a mountain of paperwork. The Chief Constable interrupted her in the task of tapping a pencil on her otherwise pristine desk whilst thinking.

"Nice tune choice, Shona. I'm rather fond of Scotland the Brave myself."

"Sorry, Sir. Thank you for coming."

He reached over and shook her hand. "I believe we have an interview to do. You take the lead as you are up to speed with the case. I will step in if I have to. If that's all right with you?"

"Of course, Sir."

"Is there anything I need to know before we go in there?"

She brought him up to date. "Very interesting. Good work, Shona." He stood back and ushered her through the door. "Let's go and interview our celebrity."

37

Once they were all seated, including the Chief, Shona thanked Louis for coming and rattled off the preliminaries for the tape.

"Thank you for coming Mr Starkind. I know you are very busy."

"I am always happy to help the police, dear girl. I am not sure why you can't do this during the normal working day."

Shona gritted her teeth. She glanced at the Chief Constable. He was gazing at Louis, an enigmatic look on his face.

She ploughed on. "I am investigating several murders. I am sure you will appreciate the urgency."

"They will be no less dead tomorrow." Louis crossed one leg over the other and leaned back in the chair. "Interrupting my dinner plans will not change that."

"Sir, your son is lying on a slab. I do feel there is some measure of urgency. More people have died. One would assume you would be worried about your own safety if nothing else."

The look of a serpent flickered across his face. He licked his lips. "Of course I'm worried. Everyone is. But telling everyone about it isn't going to help."

"Talking to me might." She changed tack. "What was your relationship like with your son?"

"Haven't we already gone through this?"

"Not to my satisfaction. Now, what was your relationship like with your son?"

"We barely had anything to do with each other. He was a horrible, useless little boy and grew up to be an even more useless adult."

"I heard he was a brilliant actor."

"Who told you that? That so called best friend of his? He'd say anything. I'm sure they were in each other's pants."

"If you do not have any evidence of that I would advise you not to say it." She consulted her notes. When she had let the silence go on for long enough she said, "Several sources have said you bullied your son relentlessly."

Louis slammed his fist down on the table. "How dare you!"

Shona jumped, leant back slightly and then bent forward. "Do not do that again. Let's keep this civil." By this point she didn't care what either of the bigwigs sitting beside her thought.

"The word on the street is that you stopped him getting any decent acting jobs. Rumour has it you were jealous of him."

Louis leaned forward. "You pig-ignorant woman. That's a pack of lies."

The Chief Constable stepped in. "Mr Starkind, you will treat my officer with respect." He leaned back in his chair again. He indicated that Shona should carry on.

"I am not answering any more questions without my lawyer present."

"Interview stopped at 19.34 at the request of Mr Starkind that he have a lawyer present."

"I will be talking to the Prime Minister about this."

The Chief Constable said, "Both the Prime Minister and the First Minister of Scotland are aware that you are being interviewed. Inspector, please take Mr Starkind to a phone so that he can ring his lawyer."

Shona deposited Louis in an office with a phone. She grabbed a passing PC and asked them to keep an eye on him. Then she sent the team home. Iain just shook his head when she went into his office. "It'll be tomorrow, Ma'am."

"Thanks, Iain. Go and see that girlfriend of yours."

"How did you kno—?"

"I know everything. Keep a clear head now."

Shona provided Louis with coffee and biscuits. The PC kept him company while they waited for Margaret McCluskey to arrive. The Chief and the Chief Constable took her down to the canteen for a sandwich. They insisted she have something to eat.

"You handled yourself well in there, Shona. Thomas was just telling me how proud he is of you. He says you're a real asset to the team."

Thomas was her boss, the Chief Inspector. His adulation for her came as a complete surprise. She managed to gather herself together enough to mutter a weak, "Thank you, Sir. I do my best."

The Battleship McCluskey was in fine form. "My client says you have been bullying him."

"Me bullying him? That's rich considering he called me an ignorant pig of a woman. Not only is that insulting but it's also misogynistic."

"I would say my client was provoked into saying this."

"Feel free to watch the video later, you will find out that is not true. Now please let me interview my client. I am sure we would all like to get home tonight, your client included."

She turned to Louis. "So you are saying these allegations of bullying are not true?"

The waiting had obviously given him time to think. "I was strict with him, yes. I had to be. His mother would have kept him a child forever."

"How strict? What do you mean by strict?"

"I made sure he did what he was told. I made him stand on his own two feet. He couldn't come snivelling to me for everything."

"Did you belittle him?"

"I made him aware that often what he did was not good enough. I wanted him to get better, to have drive and ambition. I wanted him to grow into a strong man. To be a man's man."

"He was certainly that, given the amount of women he slept with. What did you say about that?"

"Nothing. It was his own business."

"Did you know Sonya Chey was pregnant?" The haunted look on his face told her he knew.

"How do you know that?"

"It was common knowledge. She was telling everyone."

She gave him a minute to take that in. His eyes were darting everywhere. Shona sprung the trap. "She was also telling everyone she didn't know whether it was yours or Martin's."

"How dare that whore say such a thing? I wouldn't touch her if she were the only woman on the earth. Vile American."

"Louis. When you are in any station in Scotland you will not talk about women like that. Let's. keep things polite and civil." The Chief Constable's tone hinted that Louis was seconds away from being charged with racist speech or some equivalent.

"I'd also be careful about what you are saying about having sex with her. If the DNA results on the foetus come back with your DNA then you are going to be in serious trouble."

He looked at McCluskey. She whispered in his ear and he whispered back. They were like a pair of lovebirds. "My client was mistaken."

"Funny that. So what's the deal then?"

"I slept with her once, maybe twice."

"Did you know she was also sleeping with Martin?"

"I had heard that, yes."

"Yet you still had sex with her?"

"Why not? It wasn't as if she was the love of his life. Half the cast were probably sleeping with her. Men and women."

Shona gripped her hands tightly to stop herself from doing something stupid. She bit her lip hard to stop herself saying something equally daft.

"That will be all, Mr Starkind. Please do not leave Dundee. We may need to ask you more questions."

By the time she'd finished her notes and debriefed with the higher-ups it was gone 22.00 hours. All she wanted to do was go home and scrub herself in the shower. She felt grubby after Louis Starkind's filth. There were occasions when she wondered why she did this job.

Walking to the car she suddenly remembered she didn't have one. Hers was still parked outside her flat. Putting one weary foot in front of the other she went to beg a lift from Uniform. She didn't have the energy for the bus.

Entering the door she found a furious Shakespeare demanding food. She obliged her, stood in the shower and then made Belgian hot chocolate. She'd rather it was Talisker but it was a bit late to be drinking on a work night. Hangovers and detective work do not make easy bedfellows. She sat on the sofa to drink her hot chocolate. The next thing she knew it was 6 am and she had pain in her neck. She crawled into bed and set the alarm for an hour and a half later. The cat crawled on the bed with her and curled up at her back. The pair fell into a deep sleep.

38

Arriving at the station the next morning she felt like she'd had a full bottle of Talisker. Exhaustion worked just the same as whisky it would seem. This made it a fully-loaded caffeine day. She added extra grounds to the coffee maker and poured the biggest mug she could find.

Where she was going with this case she wasn't sure. She didn't know whether she wanted to arrest Shane or Louis or even both of them. Chucking both of them in cells sounded like a jolly good wheeze. The only drawback with this plan was that she'd be saddled with Runcie and McCluskey as well. She hadn't had enough coffee yet to deal with that brace of conniving, slime bag lawyers.

"Sod it, I'll wait for the Chief to arrive and he can decide."

There was a paper mountain on her desk and she made a start. She was interrupted about thirty minutes later by Nina. Interrupted having a snooze. She'd nodded off at about point fifty on the issues surrounding the road redevelopment in Tayside. She thought it might have been Forfar that did for her but she wasn't sure.

"Enjoy your kip did you?"

"I don't know how I'm going to get through today. I'll have to keep myself on the move to keep my eyelids gluing themselves shut for the duration. What brings you to my office?"

"I wondered if you fancied going to the canteen."

"No. Definitely not. If I have a full stomach I'll definitely lose the fight I'm having with my eyelids and I think the Chief Constable's still on the prowl."

"How did it go last night?"

Shona gave a brief overview and asked her to brief the others. "I take it they're all here?"

"All present and correct. Your office smells like a hospital. Are they buying cleaning supplies from Ninewells?"

"It's Deep Heat. I slept awkwardly and my neck's killing me."

"Abigail does a mean massage. You should get her on the case."

"Send her in."

Abigail appeared in her office with a towel and a small bottle of oil in her hand.

"Are you telling me you keep the essential accoutrements for a massage in your drawer?"

"Of course I do. You never know when they might come in handy."

"What for? To give a nice de-stressing massage to the Russian twins?"

"No. For Inspectors who didn't have enough brains to spend the night in their bed."

Whilst she was talking Abigail was working her magic on Shona's muscles.

"How did you work that out?"

"Because I know you. And because the way your muscles are knotted tells me the way your head was lying."

Shona fell quiet. She allowed her mind to wander and Abigail's fingers to do the work. After ten minutes her pain was gone and she felt much less tired.

"Where did you pick up that little skill?"

"My mother's a masseuse. She taught me the essentials."

"Tell your mother she's a saint."

The Chief looked worse than her if that were possible. The Chief Constable, on the other hand, looked as handsome and debonair as ever. She outlined the issues and the pros and cons of either being the killer.

They both thought for a moment. "Thomas, the decision is yours as Shona's immediate superior."

"I think, on balance, that the scales are more fully weighted on the side of Shane being our killer."

"I agree, Thomas. Whilst Louis Starkind may be an odious man that does not mean we can lock him up. Unfortunate as that may be, it is the law. Being a horrible human being does not break any laws. Not in Scotland anyway."

Shona listened to this exchange with a stunned look in her eyes.

"Get an arrest warrant, Shona. You have my full backing. I think we have enough evidence for an arrest."

"Jason. Roy. Grab stab-vests, you're coming with me."

The boys jumped up, eagerness etched into their faces like the ten commandments on tablets.

"What are we doing?"

"We're arresting Shane Martrand."

"Can we sign out guns?" Jason was doing his best impression of Charlie the King Charles spaniel.

"No you flaming well can't. We're going to do this nice and peacefully."

"Ma'am, this is you we're talking about. Peaceful disnae come into it."

"Thanks for your wise words, Peter."

She took in the bouncing DCs in front of her. "Come on you pair. Let's hustle."

In the end guns weren't entirely necessary but they would have made things a lot easier. Shane, at the first glimpse of them, took on the persona of a bare-knuckle fighter. He was staying in a serviced apartment not far from Bell Street which would have been a pleasant walk. They'd taken a squad car and a spare copper to drive them. The copper stayed in the car, like a getaway driver on a heist, parked on double yellows and with lights flashing.

Shane tried to slam the door in their faces. A well-placed size nine put paid to that idea. Unfortunately, it was Jason's size nine and he was wearing Vans. Still, it gave them a period of grace in which to shove open the door. They'd barely glimpsed the inside of the tastefully furnished apartment when Shane came at them, fists swinging. Jason and Roy leapt into action and, ducking flying fists, body tackled him to the ground. This involved a lot of yelping and wrestling around on the floor. They looked liked kids play fighting in a nursery. *Little boys grown tall.*

"What are you mothers doing to me? I'm going to kill you."

Shona applied handcuffs. In a pause between threats she said, "Shane Martrand, we are arresting you for the murder of Jedediah Ramsbottom, Della Fantine, Sonya Chey and unborn child Chey…"

By the time they yanked him up and dragged him through the door, half the remaining occupants of the building seemed to be blocking their way.

"This is disgraceful."

"All this noise. I'm trying to work."

"Why does he have handcuffs on?" This last from a blonde haired boy of about six years old.

"Could everyone please get out of our way?"

The bedlam increased. What with this and Shane's roaring, Shona had about as much as she could stomach. "Move. I'm going to count to three. Anyone still in my way after that will be arrested for obstruction."

This had the desired effect and Shane was frogmarched to the front door. Shona was ecstatic that there were only four steps to the car. Shane was thrown inside.

"Shut up. One more peep out of you and I'll find something else to add to your charge sheet."

The roaring was replaced by brooding silence. Shona liked this even less than the roaring. He was plotting something. Her sixth sense was telling her this loud and clear.

.

39

Shona was right. The minute they stepped from the car a couple of men appeared to stroll past them. With buzz cut hair and muscles on their muscles they looked like a couple of prizefighters. It fast became apparent they were ready to embrace their more thuggish side. One minute Shona was standing upright and the next full length on the cracked paving stones of the pavement. As she gathered her breath she could see the pair squaring up to batter Roy and Jason into submission. Jason neatly dodged a flying fist. The man spun round with the momentum of his throw. Jason took the opportunity and shoved him into the wall. Hard. The sound of bone on brick echoed out over the sound of city traffic. Thug number one slumped to the ground. A well aimed kick by Jason and he stayed there clutching his crown jewels.

Roy was performing what looked like an ancient pigmy dance with thug number two.

Shona caught a movement and saw Shane running, still with his hands behind his back. She scrambled to her feet and hurtled after him. A swift rugby tackle and Shane was on the ground. Shona heard a crack and then Shane started howling. "I think you've broken my leg. This is police brutality." He managed to fit this in between yowls.

"You ran away. Escaping arrest is not a bright move. You do realise that usually means an officer will try to stop you?"

More howling.

"Oh for heaven's sake, shut up. I can't hear myself to phone for an ambulance."

She called for assistance from the station then rang an ambulance. Once it arrived Jason, and a willing copper, carted him off to the hospital. Thugs 1 and 2 had been dragged into the station and thrown into cells. They were currently awaiting their lawyer's appearance. They'd have a long wait. They insisted on Margaret McCluskey who, Shona knew, was in Mull on a long weekend break.

Shona went to the ladies to check on any damage to herself or her clothes. Not too bad on either front. She would have a beauty of a bruise on her hip but otherwise fine. Her dress was now adorned with a stain. She quickly changed into the fresh one she'd brought with her that morning.

"Here the DI goes with the three changes of clothes in a day routine. Did you no' like the last little number you were sporting?" Peter had his legs stretched out and *The Courier* in his hand.

"The pavement and I had a contretemps and the concrete won."

"How come you've always got several changes of outfit about your person?" said Roy.

"Nina. Abigail."

They both looked up from their desks.

"What?"

"Have you got a change of clothes and shoes here?"

"Of course." The answer was immediate and simultaneous.

"It's a girl thing, Roy. We're ready for any eventuality."

"Here endeth the lesson. Maybe I should try that. Or maybe Jason should, as he spends a lot of time getting blood on his clothes."

"You raise a good point. Take it up with him. I'm

sure he'll be amenable to your suggestion. Peter, when you've quite finished reading the paper, I've a brace of thugs who need your attention."

"Have you seen the front of the paper, Ma'am?"

"Of course not. I've better things to worry me than the headlines."

"You might want to read this one." He handed over his well-read copy of *The Courier.*

She opened it up and her face went red.

Eminent Actor claims
police Persecution is Widespread

The Courier has been speaking to Hollywood actor Louis Starkind who claims he was arrested last night in relation to his son's murder. The grieving actor said that the way he was treated by officers from police Scotland last night was tantamount to oppression. He went on to say that he was held for several hours. "This interrogation was brutal and it was obvious the police would have liked to detain me. After several hours of interrogation I was released without charge. There was not one single solitary charge they could bring against me." Louis will be consulting his lawyer and will be suing the police. "This is not about money. It is about preventing a similar incident with someone less eloquent and affluent than myself. The police may think twice before doing the same to someone else. I feel that police time would be better sent investigating my son's murder. Time spent interrogating me means time for poor Martin's killer to get further away and evade capture. The police need to focus on what is important and leave me alone to grieve my son's death."

Shona heaved the paper in the bin. "A pack of lies and half truths. 'Poor Martin' my foot. He hated the man. Now it's all crocodile tears and feigning grief. Get that rag out of my nick."

"Of course, Ma'am." Peter pulled the paper from the bin and shoved it in his coat pocket. He'd read it at home.

"How did that blasted man get this into the papers so quickly? I thought the saying, 'Hold the Front Page' only applied to national emergencies, like we've gone to war. Not jumped-up pompous windbag actors."

"You go, Ma'am. Don't hold anything back," said Nina. Her grin softened the words.

Not quite soft enough for Shona who, eyes blazing fire, opened her mouth to utter a smart reprimand.

Peter stepped in. "You were saying something about thugs, Ma'am?"

"I was," she snapped. "Go and interview a pair who tried to assault us and kidnap Shane."

"Who'd want to kidnap that no-hope waste of rations?"

"That's what I'm hoping you'll find out in your interview. Charge them with assault to injury."

Abigail grinned. "Jason got injured again then?"

"For once it wasn't him. Our unfortunate suspect sustained a broken leg whilst they were trying to break him out."

Peter threw his head back and laughed out loud.

"Priceless, Ma'am. Truly priceless."

40

Shona rescued *The Courier* from Peter's pocket and took it along to the Chief's office. She was one hundred per cent certain he had not heard. If he had he would have stormed the bastions of her office by now. The Chief Constable was still with him.

"What do you need now, Inspector? We're in an important meeting."

"I know, Sir, and I'm sorry. I thought you would both want to see this."

She handed over the paper.

They studied it for a moment and then the head high honcho said, "Thomas, would you like to issue a reply or would you prefer I did it?"

"I think it should be me. The press need to know I have the utmost faith in my Detective Inspector and her team."

Shona took this in and tears formed in her eyes. The Chief being nice to her was almost too much to bear.

"Thank you, Sir. I appreciate your support." There was a wobble in her voice. For once she left the room thinking he wasn't that bad after all.

When she returned to her office Fagin was curled up in the corner. The dog jumped up delighted to see her.

"What are you doing here mutt? Where's your master?"

There was a note on her desk explaining that Jock had been taken into Ninewells Hospital with pneumonia. The paramedics had brought him here in the ambulance. Could Shona look after him until Jock recovered?

The answer, of course, was yes. She fondled the dog's ears. "It's been a strange old day, Fagin. I have a feeling it's going to get stranger before the day is out."

"Wuff." He licked her hand.

"So you agree. Doesn't sound good."

After arresting someone Shona usually had a sense of satisfaction and relief. This was not how she was feeling right now. The arrest did not sit easy with her. It seemed much too easy as though someone had planned it like that. She fired up a crime-mapping programme on her computer and started the process of mapping the links so far. Deep in her task the harsh ring of the phone startled her.

"DI McKenzie."

A booming voice so loud, it nearly fractured the bones in Shona's ears, winged its way out of the receiver.

Shona held it away from her ear.

"Why have you arrested one of my actors? How dare you?"

"Who is speaking please?"

"Clarissa Claris-Beauchamp. The new Director."

"Louis hasn't been arrested despite anything the papers say. I wasn't aware he was one of your actors."

"I'm not talking about that pompous fool. I'm talking about Shane Martrand."

"Shane's an actor? First I've heard of it."

"Not well known. Done some things. Taken Darren's part. Darren was Martin's understudy. I need him back."

Even more reason for him to bump Martin off.

"It doesn't work like that Mrs—"

"It's Ms, you blithering fool. Not everyone wants to be shackled to men."

Shona had a sudden urge to shackle Clarissa. To a cell door.

"—Ms Beauchamp—"

"Claris-Beauchamp. Double-barrelled. Scottish police are not very bright. Now when can I have my actor back?"

Shona pulled the phone away from her ear again. She was firmly of the opinion the woman's voice had just blown a hole in her brain. "As I was saying, it doesn't work like that. He's been charged with multiple counts of murder. He won't be out until he's found not guilty or the end of his sentence."

"When will that be?"

Are all directors as thick as this or am I just unfortunate to meet the worst of the bunch? I'd like to direct this lot into the Tay.

"About fifty years if he's found guilty."

"That's no good to me. Where will I get an actor at such short notice?"

"Ms Claris-Beauchamp, I have no idea. Go visit the Rep Theatre in town. They might have a spare one they can lend you."

"Not got time. My idiot predecessor made a right muck of things."

"I'm afraid that's not my problem." She slammed the phone down. Then she went to warn the Chief he'd be receiving a complaint about her. Fagin followed her. She was sure the little thief was planning what he could nick from the Chief's office.

She might have someone banged up for one lot of murders but she still had the poor woman found in the woods to deal with, and a missing Chinese mogul-cum-producer-cum-investor. Her brain was pounding with the thoughts swimming around inside it. She searched in her drawer for a couple of paracetamol and swigged them down with some cold coffee. Grimacing, she wandered along to the kitchen to refresh it. The kitchen looked like there had been some sort of bunfight going on. The mess made her flesh creep. While the coffee was brewing she tidied up and let her thoughts drift over the case. What was she missing? Then, in the middle of scrubbing a particularly stained mug, an idea slammed through her brain like a bullet.

41

She dropped the dirty mug in the soapy water and stripped off her Marigolds. All thoughts of coffee gone she hurried along the corridor to Iain's lair.

"Morning, Ma'am. I've—"

"Never mind the DNA for the minute. If Shane killed Della he'd be covered in her blood wouldn't he?"

"A lot of the blood might have soaked into her clothes. The furry jacket took a lot of it. But yes, the killer would have blood on them."

"Would we still be able to detect it even after a shower or bath?"

"Possibly. Under rings, jewellery, cuticles, under the nails, perhaps in the folds of the neck. I wouldn't like to stake tonight's pint on it but we might."

"Come with me."

Peter and Iain were dispatched to swab every conceivable relevant surface of Shane's skin. He was still in Ninewells Hospital A&E Department so they'd get a nice quiet cubicle and, hopefully, a nurse to help them. She asked them to come back via Shane's flat and do a search for blood there. She, and the remainder of the team, went to search the flat. The fact this had not been done until now was a measure of her level of exhaustion. Things were beginning to slip.

The flat was spacious, bright, modern and tastefully decorated. It also had the appearance of a back street slum. It would seem Shane felt that the best way to put your mark on a house was to scatter all your crap around without using any of the cupboards or drawers. This made it easier in some ways because a quick glimpse told them that ninety-nine per cent of them were empty. The remaining one per cent was filled with bottles of gin. The fridge was full of beer and a large block of cheese.

"He believed in a balanced diet. He balanced the gin with the cheese."

"That was almost funny, Roy."

"Better than you could do, Soldier Boy. It would be a balanced diet for you too."

"Boys that's enough. More searching and less chit-chat would be good."

The search threw up nothing. Every millimetre, never mind inch, of the apartment was searched even down to the inside of the air conditioning unit.

"Why have they got air conditioning in Dundee? It barely gets hot enough."

"Last year and this year have been belters, Ma'am," said Abigail. "You've got to admit it."

"It's warm but not air conditioning warm."

"There speaks Shona the original hothhouse plant," said Nina.

"I've told you before, Sergeant Chakrabarti, if you're going to insult me at least use the term 'Ma'am'."

Nina's laugh could be heard three storeys up. "Like that's going to happen, Ma'am. Anyway, I agree with you. Air conditioning in Dundee is a complete waste of money."

"You lot go back to the station. I'll wait for Iain and Peter."

To fill in the time she did another search. It still didn't throw anything up that might help them move the investigation forward.

She greeted Peter and Iain like they'd just come back from a world tour.

"We've only been gone about an hour and a half. That's some greeting."

"I've lost the will to live in here. Nothing's come up."

Iain got to work with disclosing fluid and swabs. Shona and Peter stood back and watched. He eyed up the room trying to work out where a killer might walk. Once he'd done that he opened the top of the disclosing fluid, shut the blackout curtains and looked around again. The presence of blood shows up neon bright in the dark but nothing lit up.

He moved to the other rooms and repeated the task. Not a thing showed up except for some in the hand basin in the bathroom.

"There's not much. More than likely he cut himself shaving." He swabbed it anyway.

He'd finished in less than an hour and was ready to go.

Shona walked back to the car barely picking up her feet. The worry lines on her forehead were etched deeply. Her drooping shoulders were the only sign that she was unhappy with the results. A huge glowing mass of blood would have more fully fallen in with her ability to solve the case.

Climbing in to her car she wove her weary way back to the station. She was determined to have an early knock off tonight.

42

"Iain, before I interrupted you, you were saying something about DNA?"

"The results are back in from the missing women."

"Any match?"

"Meredith Crayford."

"Thanks. I'll leave you to the swabs."

Shona set off to break the news to someone that their loved one was indeed dead. She would also have to break the news to three others that they still didn't have an answer to their loved one's disappearance.

Meredith Crayford was 42 years old when she went missing. The photo on the file showed her to be beautiful with a smile that lit up her surroundings. Her next of kin was her husband, Liam. She also had three children aged between three and seven when she disappeared. There had been a few cracks in the marriage but her husband insisted she would never leave the children. Turned out he was right. Unless he'd been the one to murder her of course.

Liam lived in a beautiful old stone house in Muirhead. This being the school holidays he was home with the children. He opened the door and Shona showed her ID card.

"DI Shona McKenzie, may we come in?"

He studied it closely then held the door open further. The house was awash with kid's toys. They could hear shrieking in the distance. He took her through to a summer room at the back of the house. Filled with stuffed sofas and bookcases, there was also a laptop open on the table. The children were running around in the garden clothed only in swimming costumes. A large paddling pool provided the reason for their attire.

The man hadn't spoken one word. He looked at them with eyes filled with fear.

Shona said, " I am sorry to have to inform you that your wife's DNA was a match to the body we found in the wood."

A flash of something in his eyes. Then they went dull. He seemed to shrivel in front of them.

"I am sorry for your loss, Mr Crayford."

"How am I going to tell the children?"

What a task. Wouldn't wish it on anyone. It's hard enough telling grown adults.

"I know this must be difficult for you, but I need to ask you some questions."

He stared at them. Then, "Of course."

"Could you tell me about the night your wife went missing?"

"I went over that repeatedly when it happened. It must be in your notes?"

"I appreciate that. I am not trying to dredge up the past but it may help us to get a fresh angle. If I hear it from you it won't be clouded by what I've read."

Abigail raised an enquiring eyebrow.

Shona shook her head. Such an infinitesimal movement it could barely be seen. Abigail interpreted and kept her mouth shut.

"That evening Meredith went out to meet some friends. It was a reunion of some of her school friends. I knew she was going to be late but when she wasn't back by 2 am I knew something wasn't right. She'd only gone out for a meal. Should have been home by 11 pm tops."

"What did you do?"

"I rang one of her friends at 2.30 am. It turned out she didn't arrive. They had a text from her saying one of the kids was sick."

"Were they sick?"

"Not that I'm aware of. The nanny didn't say anything."

"Nanny? You weren't with the kids?"

"No. I was out. Meeting a client."

Abigail interpreted Shona's look and made a note to check this out.

"What do you do?"

"I'm a ghostwriter."

"Who were you meeting?"

"This has nothing to do with the fact you found my wife's body. I'm sure I was investigated every way upside Sunday when she first went missing."

"Sorry. I agree it sounds strange. I am just trying to get a fuller picture of what happened that night."

"Who I was meeting that night had no impact on my wife's murder. I am called a ghostwriter for a reason. That reason being I sign a contract declaring anonymity."

"Did your wife have anything to do with the film industry?"

"She was an actress before we had kids. Did a few minor parts on television."

Shona's blood pumped faster. She uncrossed her legs, sat straighter and looked right at the man, a gleam in her eye.

"Did she know anyone from the film company who are currently in Dundee?"

"I have no clue. They've only been in Dundee for two months so I doubt it."

"What was your wife's last acting role, Mr Crayford?"

"She played Aladdin at The Rep a couple of years ago."

"I meant in television."

His eyes squinted as he concentrated. Eventually he said, "She was in some historical drama. It was about some laird. She was the butler's wife or something. I think it was called *Call of the Castle* or some such dross."

"Thank you. You've been very helpful. We'll be in touch if there's anything else. I am sorry to have brought you bad news."

As they walked up to the car park Abigail said, "So did his story tally up with what was said in the notes?"

"It did, practically word for word. Odd that. You'd expect discrepancies after all this time."

"I take it we're off to find out if anyone at the Discovery knows Meredith."

"You're a bright lass. I knew there was a reason you were in my team."

Shona pressed open on her car key and the doors clicked open. Within in a minute they were on their way back to Dundee.

43

Filming was in full flow. Gulls were flapping overhead and swooping down towards the man-made dock. This probably had a lot to do with the fish which they were throwing on top of a crate of artificial fish. The atmosphere was stunning. Shona could almost believe she was in turn of the 20th century Dundee.

"They're gonna regret that. They'll never get rid of those gulls now."

"But don't they bring the scene to life?"

"I'm sure the gulls were smaller in Scott's day. These lot are aspiring to be albatrosses."

A tall woman strode towards them. Her long blue and pink hair swung as she walked. Add to that a purple kaftan and she was a competing clash of colours. Without introduction Shona knew exactly who she was. The booming voice was the giveaway.

"Who the hell gave you permission to be in here? Get out now." Her huge arm was waving around in a vain attempt to summon a couple of security guards. They, knowing who Shona and Abigail were, were totally ignoring her.

"Get over here you lazy obno—"

Shona interrupted this pleasant diatribe by shoving her ID card in the woman's face. She had to stretch a bit but just about managed it.

The woman blinked and took one step back.

"DI Shona McKenzie. We spoke on the phone."

"That still doesn't give you the right to walk on to my set."

"Madam, you'll find that because I am investigating a murder I do have that right."

"It's Ms. Not a long word. You'd think you'd remember it. Still you are the filth. Not a brain cell to speak of."

"I'd be careful what you say Ms." Shona emphasised the word for good effect.

"Get out of here. Now. Do you hear me?"

"I'm sure they can hear you in Perthshire never mind Dundee. Listen to what I am saying. Carefully. We need to interview you and your crew. Is that okay?"

The woman opened her mouth but Shona interrupted.

"The next words out of your mouth had better be, "Yes, of course," or "Feel free," or I will not be responsible for my actions."

"Are you threatening me?"

"Of course not. Look," Shona's tone changed from riled to placatory, "if you let me ask each of your film crew one question we'll be on our way. We'll do any follow up after you've finished filming."

The woman, one hand on her hip, thought about this deeply for several seconds. "Fine. Start with the ones who aren't directly involved. I'll send them to you, as they're free."

"Have you got somewhere I can go?"

The woman pointed Shona in the direction of a huge camper van. "Go in there. Touch nothing."

They entered the van which was beautifully appointed and luxurious. Abigail threw herself down onto a cream leather chair.

"This is amazing. the softest leather I've come across."

Shona was busy pouring herself a coffee from a top of the range coffee machine.

"We were told not to touch anything."

"Since when have I ever paid any attention to that?

Do you want one?"

"Since never. I thought you'd never ask."

They sipped their coffee in companionable silence. There were several individual packets of luxury biscuits and a basket of fruit sitting on the table.

"I could die for a biccie. Might be pushing our luck to scarf down the victuals though."

"All this ship malarkey is getting to you, Ma'am. You've gone all nautical."

"I'm frightfully impressed myself."

"Oh frightfully. Pass more coffee darling."

"Get it yourself you lazy blighter. Get me one while you're at it."

The banter came to an abrupt halt as someone entered.

It was Felix. "Nice to see you again ladies." There was that smile again. That, and the perfectly tailored uniform which fitted his body like a glove, had the pair of them forgetting any other men existed. "What can I do for you this time, ladies?"

Shona handed him the photo of Meredith.

He studied it carefully. "Beautiful woman but I don't believe I've had the pleasure of meeting her."

"She was an actress. Mainly television. She may have been in a drama named, *Call of the Castle*."

"Not something I'm familiar with. You say *was*. Is the unfortunate woman dead?"

"She is."

"I wish you luck in finding him. All this death is a dreadful state of affairs. Thank you for all you are doing to sort this out for us."

"Blimey, Shona." Abigail fanned herself with a copy of vogue that she'd found on the table. "That man brings out my carnal side. A nice Chinese girl like myself."

"Those flashing eyes make me forget I've a man who loves me."

"Did you see his bum in those trousers?"

"Okay. Moving swiftly onwards."

The scene with Felix was repeated several times with everyone replying in the negative. Eventually one costume designer said he recognised her.

"Lovely lady. She was always so appreciative of anything we did for her."

"Do you know if she had anything to do with the film that's being shot here?"

"I don't think so. I've not seen her around. In fact, I haven't seen her in years."

It's not surprising you haven't seen her around here. She's been buried in a wood for the last eight months.

They finished up with the technicolour director.

"Never seen her in my life."

"Do you know if she had anything at all to do with this movie?"

"Not a thing. I know everyone involved."

"You've only been here two days. You can't possibly be up to speed with everything."

"I have been following this since its inception. I know everything about it."

"Can we please look through your records?"

"Over my dead body."

"That's a rather unfortunate thing to say given everything that has happened over the past few weeks."

"You are not looking at our records. They're confidential."

"Thank you for your time."

Shona stood up. Abigail swallowed the last mouthful of her coffee and followed suit.

As they strolled back to the car Abigail said, "You gave up a bit too easily methinks."

"Choose your battles my dear. That was just the first offensive. I'm going to bring in the big guns now in the form of a warrant from the sherriff."

"Tally-ho. Let's go get ourselves a warrant."

"Shona, good to see you. What sort of predicament have you got yourself into now?"

"Not a predicament but I do need a helping hand."

She outlined where they were with the investigation and why she needed to go through any records.

He thought for a moment. "How many people are you going to upset if I issue this warrant?"

"One Clarissa Claris-Beauchamp and the Alexyeyevss. Probably Ex Lord Provost George Brown as well."

"Why do you do this to yourself, Shona? And to me for that matter? Why is it that you cannot run an investigation without the Russian Mafia and Pa Broon being involved?"

Shona burst out laughing. Once started she couldn't stop.

The sherriff joined in. "You didn't think you were the only person to call him that did you? We'd been doing it for years before you came along."

"Not at all, Sir. I don't want to upset them but it's imperative that I see if Meredith Crayford had any links whatsoever to this film. Or, more specifically, the people in the film."

He thought about it for a few minutes. "I'm not sure it's the best course of action but I'll grant your request. Make sure you are discreet. Don't upset them Shona. There have been enough problems with this infernal film crew without a new stramash.

"Certainly Sir."

He wrote the warrant, signed it and handed it over.

44

"Had a nice day out, Ma'am? Wee walk along the beach was it?"

"Peter, I swear."

"I know. You can see traffic in my future."

"I can see retirement in your future."

"You'd miss me too much."

"Don't count on it." She gave the team an update on what they'd been doing and what had come from it.

"It's a bit incestuous isn't it?" said Roy. "I mean they all seem to be tangled up together and we can't separate them."

"My thoughts exactly, Roy. Each time we unravel one bit another knot appears."

"A sailor's knot I hope."

"Don't give up the day job, Jason."

"No fear. I'd miss you lot too much."

"We wouldn't miss your rubbish jokes. My niece could do better than that."

"I'd like to see you do better."

"I've had quite enough of you pair. We're running an investigation. If you like school playgrounds so much, become schoolteachers."

They shut up but glared at each other. *At least they're quiet.*

"Roy, see if you can find any connections between Meredith and the luvviess. Or any of the supporting crew for that matter. Go now."

Roy disappeared as fast as his fancy Italian leather shoes would take him.

"Jason." He perked up and looked eager.

She handed him the warrant. "Take this down to the film set and retrieve all their records. Nina can go with you." She looked around the office. "Where is Nina?"

"No' feeling well so she went home."

"What's wrong with her."

"Got the jandies," said Jason

"She's got what? Why can't you lot speak English?"

"She was vomiting. I sent her home so she didnae give it to the rest of us."

Shona shook her head. "Peter, you go with Jason. Get those records."

Peter wiped crumbs from the front of his shirt and stood up. "Come on, nae dawdling."

"Let's walk it's a lovely day."

"What have you got between your lugs? We're off to get records. If there're fifty files what do you expect we use to carry them back? Carrier bags?"

Shona smiled. She was never going to let Peter retire. He was the only sensible one amongst the lot of them. Her included.

"Abigail, bring me up to speed on what you've got on our missing Chinese gentleman."

"As I say he was highly esteemed. Despite his wealth he knew his roots. He may have a private jet but gave as much as that back to the community."

"Where did his money come from?"

"I need to go back a bit and start with where he came from. His family was dirt poor, and I mean dirt poor. They did their best but times were hard. He was often pulled out of school to beg in the streets."

"I don't mean to be racist here, but I thought the Chinese were big on education."

"They are. That's an indication of the desperation of his parents."

"So how did he go from that to billionaire?

Nothing to do with the Triads was it?"

"Not at all. It turned out young Zhou had a genius-level IQ. Despite the lack of schooling he could read, write and speak three languages fluently by the time he was ten."

Shona stood up. "Hold that thought. Call of nature."

She darted off.

A few minutes later they carried on. "You all right, Shona?"

"Yep. Too much coffee. Can we speed the tale up a bit?"

"To make the story shorter, he was reading an advanced text book that he'd half-inched from school. An influential businessman noticed and asked him what it was about. he was so impressed by the boy that he basically lifted him out of the gutter. Mr Zhou has never forgotten that."

"What are his businesses?"

"He set up a film company when he was still at school. The first film he made was a box office smash in Hong Kong. He was a millionaire in his own right by the time he went to university."

"Did he study media?"

"Business and media. Each successive film has made more than the last. He also owns a cargo shipping company and an oil company. The man is a money-making machine."

"So why did the man invest in a film company shooting a low-level movie in Dundee?"

"So he could visit his daughter and put it against tax. Simple as that. He dotes on her."

"Does anyone, anywhere have any clue whatsoever where he is?"

"The word on the street is, he's dead. Everyone

says he wouldn't disappear without letting his family know. I think it checks out."

"We need to get dogs in to search as wide an area as we can. Organise it."

"Will do. I'll start with the woods as his daughter says he loves nature."

"Whatever you think the best approach is. Ask the dog handlers. They know what they're doing. Do it tomorrow. The man's been missing for months. Another day won't hurt. Have a good evening."

45

Iain, for once, was sitting at a computer rather than dabbling about with swabs. Shona could see a spreadsheet. He was engrossed in data input.

"Iain."

No response.

Louder. "Iain."

He jumped and turned around. "Sorry. I was deep in thought."

"I can see that. What's got you thinking so hard?"

"Not one of those swabs has come back with a positive on Della's blood."

"Disappointing." *Make that disastrous. I was counting on those swabs to let us know we'd got the right man. They were going to be the cherry on top of the case against him.*

"I've been checking and double-checking where we took the swabs from. So far I think we've covered it. We even took swabs from his anal region and his groin."

"What on earth for? Thank heavens there were two of you in there."

"In case any blood had gushed on that area of his trousers. If it soaked in it might have got on his skin."

"I never thought of that."

"I did his glasses as well. Nothing on there either."

She sighed and looked resigned. "What about the swabs from the serviced apartment?"

"Again, nothing. I went back and got swabs from inside the u-bend of the sinks, the shower and the bath. There's blood down there but none of it Della's."

"Whose is it then?"

"I can't tell you exactly but I can make a best guess."

"Go for it."

"The last occupant probably had her period."

"TMI. Is there anything else we can do?"

"Not looking likely but I'll continue to collate and ponder. If I come up with anything you'll be the first to know."

"Ponder tomorrow, Iain. It's way past time for knocking off. We're all going to die of exhaustion if we don't get some rest."

She didn't have to tell him twice.

She went back to her office to see if Fagin was all right. He was nowhere to be seen. This was no surprise to Shona. The dog was probably living it up in the canteen. She popped down there but to no avail.

"He visited us earlier, Shona. He downed a plate of liver and five sausages. Then he nicked a bit of cheese off one of the PC's plates and disappeared."

She checked in all his usual haunts but no Fagin. Where could the blasted dog be? She went to break the news to the Chief that there was a mischievous dog loose about the station. There was Fagin curled up at the Chief's feet, nice as you like.

"What do you want now?"

The Chief's pride in her had obviously waned.

She thought fast. "We have the results of the swabs taken from Shane Martrand."

"They prove without doubt he's our killer?"

"I'm afraid not, Sir. They would appear to prove the exact opposite. He may not be our killer."

"DI McKenzie. Why is it you cannot run a case without it descending into chaos?"

"With all due respect, Sir. There wasn't much I could do about that. All the signs pointed to it being him. There's not much I can do tonight and we'll look at it with fresh eyes in the morning."

"Very well, Inspector. Keep me updated." He turned back to his task.

"Of course, Sir. Fagin, come. We're going home." The dog opened one eye, looked at her and shut it again. Shona could swear she heard him snore.

"Oi! Quit the acting and get up. Shakespeare's waiting to see you."

At the sound of Shakespeare's name the dog was up and at the door. His tail wagged so hard it knocked a vase off the top of a small filing cabinet. It smashed to the ground and scattered everywhere.

Shona stared in horror. She bent down and started picking up pieces of pottery. She nicked her finger and blood oozed out. She stuffed it in her mouth and sucked on it.

"Inspector, just go home. And take that animal with you. Send a cleaner up here."

"Yes Sir." She almost ran from the room, the disgraced dog at her heels.

By the time she'd finished regaling Roy, Peter and Jason with the tale they were crying with laughter. "I wish I'd seen it," said Roy.

"Instead of laughing find me a plaster. Then get those files logged into evidence and go home."

46

Despite Fagin's eagerness to see his pal, Shakespeare, Shona took the dog up to visit Jock. Strictly speaking there were only service dogs allowed in the hospital. Shona decided that the dog was in the police service and that counted. The whole of Dundee loved Jock and Fagin so the nurses turned a blind eye.

Jock's eyes lit up at the sight of his best friend. Fagin, who would usually jump up just placed one gentle paw on the covers. Jock held it. The man looked fragile. He'd lost weight.

Shona's eyes filled with tears. "How you doing, Jock?"

"Better than I was, now I'm tucked up nice and cosy in here." A coughing fit gave lie to his reassurances. An alarm went off on one of the machines. Shona looked around for a nurse.

One strolled over, and said in a calm voice. "You've dislodged the pad again." She placed a had inside his pyjama jacket and the alarm stopped. The reassuring beep reappeared.

"I'll leave you to rest and I'll take this wee thief home. Look after yourself."

She stopped at the nursing station. "How is he?"

"He's doing fine, Shona. We've got it and we'll look after him."

"Does he need anything?"

"Pyjamas, toiletries, dressing gown. Can you get into to his gaff?"

"I'll buy him new ones."

Shona's sadness at the sight of Jock meant she needed company. The company of a man and children who loved her, who would hug her and help her to laugh away her sadness. Who wouldn't care that her day had not gone as well as she had planned and would be delighted to see a sausage-stealing dog. Carrying out a normal relationship with a man who had two kids and her with a job where antisocial is the new normal could be hard and frustrating in equal measure. It was at times like this she was thankful for each and every one of them.

She knocked on the door. When it opened Douglas took one look at her and pulled her into an embrace.

"You're loved here."

The tenderness in his voice nearly brought her to tears. Screaming kids and a pair of barking dogs broke the moment. This was her life and she loved it.

47

It was easy to lure the victim to his death. To use his oversized sense of his own self-importance to ensure he was in the right place. The belief that you deserved to be the next Sir Alec Guinness, the odd hint and impression that this was possible, was impetus enough for him to be in the right place at the right time.

A short stroll through a tangle of trees and undergrowth and the figure found him waiting there in the early morning Scottish light. Lounging nonchalantly against the wall, the man had not a care in the world.

"Nice outfit, mate. Where'd you get the cloak?"

"The perfect touch I think, given the part you'll play."

"You're right there. Atmospheric."

The figure took off the cloak and hung it on a nearby branch. The man eyed it up, wondering if he could take it if it was forgotten.

"I need you to stand in various poses. To make sure that we have the right angle."

The man obliged as the figure watched. Then, the baseball bat swung towards the man's leg. He winced but did not move. The assurance it was a prop ensured his compliance in standing still. The sickening thud of wood against bone reverberated through the woods. The trees caught it and absorbed it into their branches, poisoning them with evil. Eyes widening in shock the man sank to the ground howling with the pain in his shattered leg. The bat was redeployed on the other leg. More screams, deadened by the trees. The figure was not worried. No one used this park at this time. Not many houses nearby but anyone hearing the faint echo would think it was the cry of a fox.

Another swing and the baseball bat was used time and time again. The head this time, until the man's skull was unrecognisable.

It was only then the figure donned the cloak and walked from the woods. The baseball bat was left discarded by the body.

48

Shona was late for work next day as she detoured to
Marks and Spencer's to buy everything that Jock
needed. PJs., dressing gown, slippers and socks went
into her trolley. This was followed by enough toiletries
to supply the hospital. She headed down to the food hall
and added magazines, a couple of bottles of juice,
several packets of sweets and some fruit. There was no
way Jock was lying in that hospital without someone
looking after him. Not on her watch.

Heading into the station she popped into uniform and
asked if someone could blue-light the supplies to Jock.
They were happy to oblige. "You've a warm heart,
Ma'am."

"Don't you go ruining my reputation now."

"Wouldn't dream of it."

Her office smelt of lavender polish. Mo's signature
smell. She'd obviously returned from compassionate
leave. She put the dog in the corner and told him to
stay. Fagin's look said *Yeah right*. The minute you're
out the door I'm gone. She put one foot out of the door
to find out what the others were up to, when the phone
rang. She hurried back inside.

The minute she heard the duty sergeant's voice she
knew it did not bode well.

"There's a wee lassie wants to speak to someone
important. Someone she was told to give info to. Says
the papers said so."

"Is she on her own?"

"Her dad's with her. She won't tell him either.

Says it's got to be you."

"Bring them up."

The wee lassie turned out to be about fourteen, articulate, bright and had Down's Syndrome. Shona introduced herself and explained they would need to record the interview.

"I don't mind. I thought that would happen. We did a law unit at school."

"She's got more brains than me this one." Her elderly father rubbed his stubble with work worn hands. "I've no clue what the problem is but she insisted on seeing you. I left work to bring her here."

"May I ask your name?"

"Morag Gillespie. I'm fourteen. I've got information for you Detective Inspector Shona McKenzie."

"Thank you for bringing it to me. What's the information?"

"I think there's someone dead in Camperdown Park."

Her father jumped to his feet. "Morag, why didn't you tell me? Why didn't you ring the police from your mobile?"

"It's all right Mr. Gillespie, I've got it."

"The paper said anyone with information should speak to you. I came straight here."

"You did right Morag. Where in the park was it?"

"At the back. Beside the wall."

"What were you doing there lassie?"

"One of the baby ducklings ran away. I was trying to get it back to its mummy."

"She loves animals. Cannae bear to see them hurt."

"So fairly near the pond then? Could show us?"

"Yes. I know where it is."

She picked up the phone. "Peter, possible dead body in Camperdown Park. Get squad cars. We've two extra passengers. Call the POLSA as well. Tell him to meet us there."

The excitement on Morag's face at being in a squad car going at full pelt and with sirens blaring made Shona smile. She couldn't remember when she last had that adrenaline rush. Now all she got was a sick feeling in her stomach at the waste of life. The car stopped as close to the pond as possible and Shona jumped out. Immediately a few onlookers appeared.

"Move back as far as the café."

"We've got a right to be in this park," said one young man. He had tattoos and piercings all over his face. "I'm walking my dog."

The elderly boxer looked quite pleasant compared to its hostile owner.

"You can walk it to your little heart's content in the other direction. You can't go this way; you'll frighten the ducks."

"Are you saying my dog would go after the ducks?"

"No, I'm saying the sight of you is enough to scare them off. Now shove off before I arrest you."

He stomped off muttering obscenities. "Charming young man," she said to the air. Everyone else had disappeared in the direction of the body.

Shona caught them up. There was indeed a dead body. The very dead body of Darren Spottiswood with his head caved in. The wall was decorated with copious amounts of blood and what Shona was sure was brain tissue.

"We should get the wee lassie out of here. It's no' nice for her to see."

Shona glanced over at the wee lassie. She looked quite unperturbed given this was the second time today she had seen this. The father on the other hand...

"Get the pair of them out of here. Take them down to the zoo. Ask if we can use their education room as a centre of operations."

Peter ushered them off reassuring Mr Gillespie he could have a nice cup of tea when he got to the zoo.

Shona made everyone stand back until the POLSA arrived and took control. He was there ten minutes later with all the equipment to secure the scene. Shona watched as he expertly sealed off the area and moved any bystanders well back. So far back they couldn't see anything other than the trees. There was the usual mutterings about infringement of freedom and police persecution. Shona was immune to them. She'd heard it all so many times she could recite them in her sleep.

While she waited she examined the image of the crime scene, which was frozen onto her brain.

49

It took about half an hour before the POLSA was ready to release the crime scene to her and the team. They used the time to get fully kitted up in coveralls and masks. Shona indicated only she and Iain should go initially. Like a couple of survivors of the apocalypse, they entered the area. Sunlight flickering through the branches threw eerie shadows in a fractured dance around the scene. This made it difficult to search with any accuracy. The moved slowly looking at the ground and all round them for any evidence.

Close up the body looked worse than she first imagined. Darren was dressed in a sailor's uniform. Like Jedediah his legs were shattered and he had bones sticking through the material of his trousers. Yet again this was someone who meant business. This was personal and went beyond death. It was rage in its purest form. Whoever did this had anger oozing from every pore.

Iain was busy using close up, macro and telephoto lenses, changing them swiftly and expertly to get the perfect shot. Small and wiry he was light on his feet. Despite the apparent concentration on photos he maintained focus on the ground making sure not to destroy evidence. A telephoto lens was brought into play to take a photo of the blood and possible brain matter on the grey, dry stane dyke that supported the victim.

"What a way to end your life," he said.

"You're not wrong. The pain Darren must have felt would have been unimaginable. To start with that is. He'd have been unconscious and then dead in fairly quick succession."

She stayed pretty much in one place allowing Iain to get all the photos he needed before she disturbed any evidence. Despite her relaxed pose she was taking in every detail of the crime scene. The murder weapon was obvious given it was lying next to the body. She wondered why the murderer was no longer disposing of the weapon elsewhere. *Either a sign of the killer's growing confidence or he was taunting them. Probably both. When I get my hands on them I think I'll employ a baseball bat to their skull.*

Iain finished up and she was free to roam.

"Did you find anything of note?"

"Some depressions in the undergrowth that could be footprints. The ground's not as hard here as the tree canopy protects it from being baked by the sun."

"It's a public park. Could be anyone back here."

"True. Let's hope it's good news."

"Yeah, right. This is me we're talking about."

"You raise a fair point, Ma'am. Probably half of Dundee and a good bit of Perthshire has been trampling around this bit of park." His wide smile took the sting from the words.

"You're a cheeky boy. Go let the others in."

50

The others were not happy.

"It's hotter than Hades in the suits. While you've been in the cool of the trees we've been out here sweating like bulls at the sight of a cow in heat.."

"Nina, you can be a right big girl's blouse at times. Go get a job in an office with air conditioning. At least you won't be giving me all sorts of grief."

"She's got a point. I've lost aboot five pounds in weight."

"At least your wife will be happy. Would you lot stop moaning and get some work done?"

"Would you like us tae do a search?"

"Feel free. Start inside then fan out and do a wider search. I'll grab a few uniforms to help."

Brian Gevers leapt at the chance to join them. "It'll get me in fine fettle for when I join your team."

"Do you know something I don't?"

"No, Ma'am, but I'll be in it one day."

"I would be happy to have you. Go and report to Sergeant Johnston." He left at a rapid clip. It was nice to see someone so happy in his task. He wouldn't be quite so chirpy when he donned coveralls and mask on top of his uniform. It would completely dampen his enthusiasm for a gig with CID.

The serious search was now underway and they all got down to business. Every inch of the ground and up to head level of the tree canopy was searched. Inch by painstaking inch they covered the terrain. Bottles of water were brought and downed like it was the elixir of life. Given the temperatures it was certainly necessary for life. Having most of the team in hospital with dehydration tended to slow an investigation down.

A slip of paper was placed in an evidence bag. A cigarette end, some threads of cloth from a tree. All were bagged and handed to the POLSA to go into evidence. After an hour of concerted effort Shona informed the team she was off to interview Morag.

"Nina, you can come with me." The lass still didn't look too sparky after her bout of vomiting. Her pale face worried Shona. She wanted to get Nina into the cool and get some fluids inside her.

Shona took off her mask, pulled her hood down and grabbed four bottles of water and four bottles of coke from the cafe. Also some biscuits and a couple of bags of sweets. She reassured them that she would be back to pay the minute she could get to her money. They assured her she could have them for nothing. Any of the police could.

She took her spoils of war into the education centre and dumped them on the table.

"Help yourself. Nina, get some coke inside you, and a couple of biscuits."

Nina reached for the bottle and slugged some down. She looked marginally better now she was out of the sun. Shona felt bad for having snapped at her earlier. She watched Nina pull the wrapper off a couple of digestives.

Morag was drinking her coke and munching on a peanut butter cookie.

"Morag, you were very brave to come and report that to us. You did the right thing."

"I do what I'm told. It told me what to do in the paper."

"I know, and I'm glad you did. May I ask you some questions?"

"Yes. You always answer a policeman's questions.

Daddy says so."

"Thank you. What time was it when you saw the dead body?"

"Eight thirt-four am. I looked at my phone. On the telly the police always do that."

Phone! A lightbulb flashed in Shona's brain. "Did you take any photos?"

"Yes."

"May I see them?"

The lass had taken three photographs. They were a bit grainy but Shona got a good impression. These would be supporting evidence.

"The phone will need to stay with us for a little while, Morag. We need to get the photos from it."

"Daddy says I've always got to keep my phone on me. I can't give it to you."

"It's okay. Morag. You can use mine."

Morag beamed at Shona. The issue had been resolved. She handed over the phone. Nina pulled an evidence bag from her pocket and dropped the phone in it.

"You didn't share any of this online did you?" Shona's voice had an urgent inflection.

"No. I don't put photos online. Daddy told me not to."

Shona was beginning to think Daddy was a jolly wise man. *I wish all daddies were like him. Mind you not all teens are as compiasnt as the amiable Morag. Most daddies would give in at the first sign of a petulant strop.*

"What did you first see when you came across the dead man?"

"I thought he was ill. I went to see if I could help."

"Did you touch anything?"

"No. I got scared when I saw all the mess. I ran away." The girl's lip trembled. The first sign of distress

Shona had seen. She'd taken more on board than she exhibited.

"That's all right, Morag. That's what I would have done. Not touching it was good."

A glimmer of a smile reappeared on her face.

"Did you see anyone else when you were in the park?"

"No. Just the baby duckling. Will it be all right? It needs its mummy."

"We've returned it to its mummy. It's happy swimming in the pond."

The beam was back.

"We don't have any more questions for you Morag. It was really nice to meet you."

"Can I go back to the pond to see the ducklings?"

"Not at the moment. Sorry."

Taking in the distress on his daughter's face, Mr Gillepsie said, "I'll take you to Vissocchi's for an ice cream. You can have as many scoops as you want."

The wonder in her face gladdened Shona's heart.

"Can I have four?"

"For today, yes. We're back to normal tomorrow."

"I want chocolate, toffee, raspberry, and banana. No wait, maybe I'll have…"

The smile her father gave Shona was wry. He thanked her and bore his daughter off for her treat.

This day was going to cost him dearly in more ways than one. Shona had no doubt that the girl would need counselling sometime in her future. No normal person could see the sight in those woods and not be affected. The police, of course, were not normal.

"Nina, stay here in the cool and get some fluids down you. Get more water from the café."

Nina, looking much more like her old self said, "Thanks. Ma'am. That would really be great." Showing a glimmer of her usual spunk she said, "You're a top boss, Shona McKenzie."

51

Peter was mopping his brow under the headgear when she returned to the crime scene.

"How come none of us are affected by a sight like this? I find it worrying that it's all in a day's work."

"That's why it doesn't affect us, Shona. It's because it's work. We're too busy focusing on catching a killer than how horrible the corpse looks."

"It's not very compassionate."

"Turning off your mind to horror doesn't mean you're not sad for the death. It means you're a professional who wants to help the victim in the only way you can."

"You're a very wise man, Peter Johnston."

"Unfortunately I came about that wisdom the hard way. I found it difficult to switch off when I was younger. In the end I had to do it for the sake of the wife. When the kids came along it was even more necessary."

"Well, I never knew that."

"It's not something I broadcast to be honest. I was ashamed of it. But not now."

"I admire you for admitting it. You're a strong man."

Shona had a feeling that his putting his feet up and reading the paper was his way of dealing with the horrors. Wrapped up inside a news item they didn't seem half as bad. It gave him down time and a chance to refresh. She had the utmost respect for him already but it went up sevenfold after this conversation.

"Och away with you." Peter was back to his normal jocular self. "You'll have me in tears in a minute."

It was time to leave the conversation behind.

"Where's the search going?"

"All over the park."

"Ha ha. You know what I mean."

"There was a tyre print found outside the park. Looked like a car was parked just outside the barrier at the side gate. The one that goes from the Birkie Inn to Asda."

"Could it have been a car turning?"

"That's what I thought but Iain says no. He thinks a car was parked there."

"There are some houses over the road aren't there? Check if the car belonged to them."

Peter found Jason and dispatched him in the direction of the houses. The lad hotfooted it.

"Does he think he's still in the Army? We don't have to double time everywhere in Dundee. It's no exactly Afghanistan." His words were accompanied by a mopping of the brow on the sleeve of his coverall.

"Getting your DNA over your clothing isn't the brightest of moves."

"Getting my sweat all over the crime scene might not be the brightest of moves."

"Peter, you're a genius." She darted off leaving Peter standing with a puzzled look on his face.

She found Iain directing a couple of tame coppers.

"Iain, how easy would it be to check for droplets of sweat around here?"

"Nigh on impossible, Ma'am." The look on his face said she was addled but he was too polite to say it. "Have you seen the size of the area? We'd not finish this side of Christmas."

"What about the immediate area around the body, the body itself and the baseball bat?"

He thought for a minute, scratched the side of his face through the coverall, thought again and said, "I'll give it my best shot."

"Do you need any help?"

"Send Roy. He's quite methodical."

"He's all yours. Do you want my help"

"I think we'll manage. I'll find Abigail if I need an extra pair of hands."

"I'll see you back at the station."

She made her way back to the squad car and climbed in. Her return to the salt mines was more sedate and accompanied by Radio 2. She belted out a few accompanying vocals for the songs that came over the airwaves.

52

The impromptu karaoke lifted her mood. It came crashing down when she realised she needed a trip to Riverside and the film set. She had the unenviable task of breaking the news to Ms Clarissa Claris-Beauchamp that another one of her actors was dead. She downed a mug of coffee and a couple of preventative paracetamol. This should deal with the headache she knew she was going to have at the sound of Clarissa's voice.

She borrowed a PC from her disgruntled oppo in Uniform.

"You seem to think every copper in this nick is at your beck and call."

"Sorry, Steve". She was hoping his name was Steve. The previous incumbent of the post had moved to Aberdeen. Steve, or whatever his name was, had only been in post a month. "All my guys are currently in Camperdown dealing with a particularly vicious murder."

"Okay, but don't make a habit of it."

I really need to take this guy out for a drink and get him to loosen up a bit. He's going to get a bit of a shock when he realises just how often I purloin his bobbies.

Brain Gevers still being along at the park she was loaned a delightful chap called Bernard. He'd come late to policing but loved it. He was delighted to be going to a film set. Shona was convinced he wouldn't be quite so delighted when he met Clarissa. They took advantage of the lovely weather and walked down in ten minutes. It was quicker than finding the car and negotiating the new road system.

Clarissa had to be woken from a nap to speak to them. She was sporting a fluorescent green kaftan today. For some strange reason it had pink spots around the hem. The woman was a walking talking kaleidoscope. The fact that she'd been woken up meant her voice went from booming to off the stratosphere.

"Stop bothering me. You've arrested the person responsible for the deaths. Get out now. You don't have permission to be here."

Shona shuddered in the sonic boom.

Bernard just looked shocked. He was staring at Clarissa, eyes wide with fascination.

"I don't need permission. I'm investigating a murder. Now is there somewhere we can talk?"

"I'm not talking to you lot. Now shove off and get off my set. You're trespassing."

Shona's voice was low but striped with steel. "We either speak here or at the station. Now which is it going to be?"

Clarissa weighed her options, then, "Come with me."

She led them back to the van.

Shona eyed up the coffee but it was not to be.

"Get on with it. I've things to do."

"That's funny. We were told you were having a nap when we arrived. Doesn't sound very busy to me."

"You are one of the rudest people I've met. Are all police this hostile."

"Only the ones that have to deal with you," Shona muttered under her breath."

"What did you say?"

"I said, not usually, maybe one or two."

"You're obviously one of them."

"I'd advise you not to insult me any more. As a

223

police officer there is only so much I can take before I arrest you and chuck you in a cell."

The woman glared at them. She leaned forward and placed her huge arms on the table. If she was trying to be intimidating it was wasted on Shona. At least she'd stopped shouting.

"Do you know where Darren Spottiswood is?"

"No t a clue. I'm not his mother. He's not filming today. He's not attached to my breast."

Shona was busy praying that Felix would come in and cheer her up.

"Have you got a phone number for his next of kin?"

"What for? What's he done?"

"Nothing as far as we are aware. However, I am sorry to have to inform you he is dead."

"Dead? How? What am I going to do with another one of my actors lying on a slab?"

"We have reason to believe it is murder."

"How can it be murder? The murderer's locked up in your jail."

Shona had been thinking about that very same issue. She was not happy with the conclusion it led her to. There was a conversation with the Chief in her future.

"That is something we are looking into."

"This is all Xavier Lovelady's fault. He has brought a curse on this film."

"Where is Mr Lovelady? No one seems to have seen him in days. Since you arrived in fact."

"Probably ran off with his tail between his legs. Odious man."

"I take it there is no love lost between you both?"

"Correct. The man calls himself a director. He is an insult to the name."

"Why do you hate each other so much?"

"Nothing to do with you. Or your investigation. Mind your own business."

She made a valid point. However, Shona intended to find out exactly what the deal was between these two.

"When did you last see Darren?"

"Yesterday. Doing some evening filming. Rushed off the minute he'd finished filming. Said he had to meet someone."

"Do you know who?"

"Some whore probably. There's plenty of groupies hanging around. They'll sleep with anyone."

"Do you know any of their names?"

"Of course not. Do I look like someone who's interested in a load of groupie whores?"

Shona thought she'd better end the interview before she smashed this one in the teeth. The urge was strong that she curled her fingers inside her closed fist and pressed her nails hard into her palm.

"That will be all. I will need to interview the remainder of your film crew. Please make them available."

"You're not doing it in here."

"That's absolutely fine. We will invite them all to the station and do the interviews in the comfort of one of my interview rooms."

"Preposterous. That will stop my filming for the day."

"Absolutely. However, I would not want to inconvenience you by doing the interviewing here."

"You're blackmailing me. I'll put in a complaint."

"Please do. You'll find the contact details for the police Investigations and Review Commissioner on the Internet. On the other matter I am not blackmailing you. I am merely pointing out the options."

"So you're saying you want to interview everyone

here?"

"I'm not saying any such thing. I'm saying I need to interview them here or at the station."

"I suppose you'd better do it here then." The woman heaved her huge bulk out of the chair.

"No so fast. Let's start with you."

"Me? I've had nothing to do with it."

"Let me be the one to decide that."

"Stupid woman. I wasn't even here when the first murders happened."

"Just exactly where were you?"

"At my holiday home in the Dordogne."

"So, where were you between the hours of 2 am and 4 am last night."

"With my lover."

"And he is?"

"She is and it has nothing to do with you."

"Look, I don't care which sex your lover is. I just need to check your alibi." Shona clutched the edge of the table to stop herself throwing herself across it and strangling this woman. *I wish someone would murder her.*

"Annabelle Bertram-Smith."

Bernard jotted down the name.

"Where might I find her?"

"In the serviced apartments above the casino."

"The same place that Shane Martrand lived?"

"Yes. That's not a crime is it?"

"No. Thank you, that will be all."

"Are all actors as horrible as her?"

"She's not an actor ,she's a director and you're right she is horrible. I'm wondering if I could run her through with a cutlass and get away with it."

His eyes lit up. "Can I do it, Ma'am? I'd do the jail time for it."

"The likes of her aren't worth losing your career over. In their world, everyone is on an ego trip."

They repeated the same interview over and over. Each and every actor or support personnel had an alibi. It was going to be door to door and checking those alibis, over and over.

Shona told Bernard he was free to go. "You'll miss out on the boring bits. Plus it will just be more idiots lying through their teeth. Then we'll need to sort through the lies to get to the truth."

53

When she returned the team were back, exhausted and hungry. She sent for several extra-large pizzas and donated some of them to Uniform. She felt she ought to build a few bridges with Steve. She still wasn't sure he was actually called Steve but he hadn't said otherwise. She needed him on side so she could borrow his coppers at will. He was right when saying she thought his coppers belonged to her.

"I know you're all weary to your marrow but it's time to get your feet on the ground again."

Ghosts could have used the collection of groans on a good day.

"My feet haven't recovered from earlier."

"Your feet barely touched the ground earlier, Nina. You were sitting in the café."

"Somebody's got to do it." She'd recovered and was back to her old bouncing self. "I'll lead the charge on this one. Who's with me?"

They sorted themselves into pairs and disappeared. Shona had kept Roy behind to do some searches on 't'internet'.

She briefed him and walked down to evidence.

"I need the files that we logged in yesterday."

The woman behind the desk obliged. "Do you want me to help you upstairs with these?"

"You're an angel."

There still weren't enough hands so Shona press-ganged Mo. She put down her Hoover and picked up a couple of bags.

Safely deposited in her office she picked up the first file. She was halfway through the second file looking for links to Meredith Crayford when she suddenly remembered something.

She dashed into the Chief's office.

"Shona, it's polite to knock."

"Sorry, Sir. There's been a development." She outlined everything that had happened that day.

The Chief went quiet. Not his usual 'I'm about to explode and shoot you' quiet. More a thoughtful, deep sort of silence.

Shona waited it out.

"It looks like we are going to have to release Shane Martrand."

"He may have done the others, Sir."

"It's highly unlikely there are two killers using the same MO and targeting the same film crew."

"I don't know, Sir. They've probably upset most of Dundee by now." She smiled.

The Chief smiled back. This was the first time she'd seen this so it took her by surprise.

"You're probably right but I still think we need to release our prisoner. I will inform the Chief Constable."

"Thank you, Sir. There's only one problem."

"Which is?"

"Our other major suspect was Louis Starkind."

"You cannot arrest him. We'll have the Prime Minister on the phone to the First Minister. It might catapult us in to another independence debate."

"I will at least have to interview him as to his whereabouts last night."

"I agree. Call me when you have him in and I will be in the interview with you."

"It may take some time, Sir. I'm not sure he's around."

"Where exactly is he?"

"He took a plane to London this morning."

"Get him back. Now. He was told not to leave."

"Advised, Sir. I'm not sure the PM would be happy with us telling his best friend to do anything."

"Just get him back."

Shona phoned the Met Police and asked them to get Louis back on a plane to Scotland. They were somewhat taken aback. "We can't arrest Louis Starkind."

"For heavens sake don't arrest him. Just make sure he gets on the plane. We've a few questions to ask him."

"Can't we do it for you?"

"Unfortunately it's part of a bigger case so it has to be us. Shame really as I'd love to foist him on you. Have you ever met Louis?"

"No, I'd love to. He's my heart-throb. Did you see him in 'A War to Die For'?"

"I can't say I did. Trust me once you've met him your heart won't be throbbing quite so much. You'll be reaching for a noose."

She thanked her, hung up, and went to release Shane from his shackles.

54

Shane's incarceration had not changed his personality any. He was still a thug and still roaring fit to wake the dead.

"I'm going to sue you effing b—"

"Stop right there."

"Why? Why should I listen to anything you lot say? You framed me."

"You what? Are you as thick as you look? We arrested you because the evidence pointed to you being the killer. You can't sue us for that."

"How am I meant to get home?"

"You can practically see your apartment from here. It's a two-minute walk."

"I'm a star. I don't walk."

"Oh for goodness sake, wrack off and leave me alone. Go home and go back to your part. I don't think they've had time to recast your role."

This got him out of the door quicker than anything.

A couple of hours later the read pile of the files was bigger than the unread. Progress was being made but not on the case. Nothing. Nada. Zilch. No connection between Meredith and anyone in Pink Play Productions. Shona rubbed her head and took a mouthful of coffee. Cold. The team was still missing in action. She was rather hoping they'd gone to the pub and she could join them. A nice crisp, cold Chardonnay would slip down quite nicely right about now.

Instead of a Chardonnay she got Adanna Okafor.

"How did you get in here? Get out now."

"That's no way to treat an old pal."

"Old pal? You're lucky you're not in the stocks

231

right now."

"Why, what have I done?"

"That pack of lies you wrote about us mistreating Louis 'The God' Starkind."

"That wasn't me. I was off that day visiting my sick grandmother. Dear old Granny had a fall and I was the designated relative to go take her up the hospital."

"So who did write it?"

"Caleb Brown. He's a nasty little man. Even the rest of the journos hate him."

Shona still wasn't convinced about Adanna's innocence but decided to give her another chance.

"How's your granny?"

"Fine. Lots of bruises. She's moaning she can't play tennis."

"She sounds a bit like my gran. We should get them together. Though I think she's disappeared off to Tibet or somewhere like that."

"Kudos to her. Your granny sounds like my sort of woman."

"Enough talk of aging relatives. What are you doing here?"

Adanna opened her mouth to reply.

"No. Scratch that. 'How did you get in here?' is a more important question."

"I've several relatives who work in the station. They let me through."

"Who are they? Heads are going to roll. We can't have unescorted civilians wandering round the place."

"I wasn't unescorted. My cousin dumped me outside your door and ran off."

"I bet he did."

Adanna's laugh rattled around the office.

"What exactly do you want?"

"A scoop."

"Do you not give up? How many times have I told

you I don't do scoops?"

"You can't blame a girl for trying. What's happening up at Campie?"

"You'll find out when we have a press conference."

"If that means there's another dead body your suspect in the cells can't be the murderer."

"You should join the police. You obviously think you can do it better than us."

"Not a chance. You lot get shot at and stuff. My granny needs me."

"I need my granny. She'd be better at this than me. She'd take one look at the lot of them and say Louis Starkind did it because his granny refused to give him a dummy when he was wee."

"She's probably right. Not about Louis Starkind but about the dummy."

"If I give you a minor scoop will you shove off and leave me alone?"

"With pleasure."

"We've released Shane Martrand without charge."

She was up out of her chair and through the door before Shona could say 'Escorted'. Shona followed her to make sure she went straight to the front door and didn't pass Go.

55

Almost back to her office she broke into a sprint and grabbed the ringing phone.

"It's Petra here from the Met police."

"Is Louis safely on the plane?"

"He is. Thank goodness. I now know what you mean about him being a complete bar steward."

"No throbbing heart now then?"

"Not a throb to be seen."

Peter and Iain were the first back.

"My feet are killing me. I'm too auld for this. It's the youngsters should be traipsing about the town talking to people."

"I agree, Peter. Please feel free to take it up with the Chief. I'm sure he'll be fascinated."

"It wouldn't be so bad if we'd come up with anything," said Jason.

"A fruitless search then?"

"Barren, Ma'am."

The other two teams said the same. All they'd come up with was a suntan. All alibis checked out.

She sent the bulk of the team home but kept Roy. "Now that you're all grown up you can cope with a late knock-off."

"'Sup?"

"Do you have to talk like a teenager?"

"It means I'm down there with the kids, Ma'am."

"You may not have noticed but I'm not a kid. Did you come up with anything on the feud between Louis and Clarissa?"

"Not much. There were a couple of times when they resorted to fisticuffs. These were widely reported in the media."

"That's a bit extreme even for that lot."

"Word on the street says they were publicity stunts. I'm not so sure."

"Why's that? Talk me through your thinking."

"They've known each other a long time. I get the impression they've got history over and above being rivals in movies."

"Rivals in love maybe. Mind you, whoever they were fighting over would have to be bisexual. Our Clarissa bats for the other team."

"There's no whisper of that. Are you sure?"

"Got it from the mare's mouth herself. She's not that fond of men. Could you grab someone from Uniform and go and pick up Louis from Dundee Airport? Don't take any crap off him. Your position usurps his connections, any day of the week."

"Okay. Sweet."

"After I've interviewed him you and I are off to the pub."

"Is this a date?" An evil grin lit up his face.

"You should be so lucky. We're off to the Rabbie to listen to the scuttlebutt. Our guru is probably there as well. I need a word with him."

"Is the firm paying for our drinks?'

"Out of the Chief's purse strings? No way. I'll buy you a pint. I might even throw in a sausage roll."

"That seals the deal, Ma'am. A drink, gossip to listen to and one of Alex's missus's homemade sausage rolls. Sounds like the perfect night. Oh, and a date with you of course."

"Cheeky git. If this is a date how come I'm paying?"

"Equal opportunities, Ma'am."

Her laugh could be heard in the Chief's office. She swatted him away with a wave of her hand.

"Shoo. Go fetch Louis."

Laughing, Roy went off to obey the command.

56

To say Louis was furious would have been the understatement of the millennium. It was white-hot fury which had got itself up to full temperature ready to brand anyone who got in its way.

"How dare you? How dare you?"

"Thank you for coming back Mr Starkind." She leaned back in her chair. "To be honest I'm surprised you left in the first place."

"I'm a free citizen. I can go anywhere I want."

"Not when we asked you politely to stay local. That was actually a euphemism for don't leave Dundee or we'll drag you back."

"Detective." The Chief's voice was low but she grasped its meaning. Back off.

"Let's stay civil, Louis. That way we can get the interview over and done with. Then we can all go home. Home somewhere in Dundee that is."

"I refuse to be civil towards you. You are an obnoxious, jumped-up, rude girl, who doesn't know her place."

"Thank you for clearing that up. My place is in this nick. I can quite easily allow you to enjoy my hospitality by arresting you. For no other reason than you're a horrible human being. That and for hate crime for the way you've just spoken to me."

The Chief tensed and glanced at her but left her to it. He was getting ready to lambast someone. Whether it was her or Louis Shona wasn't quite sure.

"Where were you between 2 am and 4 am this morning?"

"Where everyone is, in bed."

"Is there anyone who can prove this?"

"Some prostitute that I ordered online."

"Can you produce this mysterious prostitute?"

"Of course not, she was just good for sex."

"The name of the online ordering service?"

"No clue." He crossed his legs and assumed a bored look. "Is this going anywhere? I haven't got time to sit around for hours because you can't do your job properly."

"I have had quite enough of you talking to my Inspector like that. Do it again and I will arrest you. You will answer her questions and do it with respect."

"I agree, Chief Inspector." The Chief Constable had entered the room. "I will give you my full backing and that of the First Minister."

There's going to be some sort of diplomatic incident between Holyrood and Westminster before the night's out. We might be lobbing bombs at each other. All over one man who she would quite cheerfully drop into the River Tay. With concrete blocks tied to his ankles.

"You lot are far too touchy."

Shona started to rise but a light touch from the Chief Constable held her down.

"I wasn't with a prostitute last night; I was with the Alexeyevs."

The detectives all looked at each other.

Flaming Nora. How come the Kalashnikov twins are crawling all over my case again?

"Pa Broon wasn't with you, was he?"

"Who? You, my dear girl, don't half talk a load of rubbish."

Shona decided to leave it be. She'd get her revenge somehow. "Ex Lord Provost George Brown. Was he with you?"

"Dear George? No, he didn't join us."

"Wha…" Shona couldn't even finish. She was taking the mick, not asking a serious question. Could this night get any worse?

The Chief Constable took over. "Mr Starkind we would like you to stay here while we make some enquiries. Would you like a drink while you wait?"

"Drink the swill you serve here? Never."

"Very well. Please stay here. Our constable will wait with you."

"I don't need an escort."

"Yes you do. Unless, of course, you would like to wait in a cell?"

"The Prime Minister will not be happy."

"The First Minister is awaiting his call."

As they left the interview room the Chief Constable turned towards her.

"Thank you Shona, you did well. Could you please ask the Alexeyevs to come in?"

Shona phoned Peter, Jason and Iain. She broke the news she needed them to fetch the Alexeyevs. She went to find Roy. "There's going to be a bit of a delay on that date. I've to interview the Alexeyevs."

"The night is still young, Ma'am."

57

The night may well be young but Shona was definitely feeling her age. Sixteen hour shifts didn't appeal to her any more. She picked up the phone and dialled Douglas's number. She explained she wouldn't be coming round for tea as promised.

"The kids will be disappointed."

"They've got Fagin to keep them company."

She'd dropped the mutt off on her way to work. Douglas's mum had agreed to look after it. She was a saint in human disguise. Nothing fazed her. Except maybe Charlie, the puppy, who was a bit much for anyone.

The sound of Douglas's voice soothed her and reminded her why she worked so hard. To keep the streets safe for those she loved.

Douglas kept her company until the Alexeyevs arrived in the station. The interview was swift but noisy. The usual load of old Horlicks about police persecution and picking on foreign nationals. They claimed they had been with Louis. A business meeting. A bit of pushing and it turned out the business meeting had involved gambling. Not for money of course. Oh no. That would be illegal.

Yeah, right and I'm the Dalai Lama. This pair are talking right out of their very Russian backsides.

No amount of questioning swayed them from this path. They had to release Louis. This time he had a warning not to leave Dundee and not to talk to the press.

"That is an assault on my civil liberties and my freedom of speech."

"Please feel free to take this to your lawyer. We'll look forward to hearing from him or her."

"Do you think I'd have a woman as a lawyer?"

Shona had a sudden urge to shove something up his jacksy. So hard it would meet his tonsils. She kept this fact to herself. Stuff like this tended to get you in bother.

"If you need a local lawyer I am sure Margaret McCluskey would be happy to help. She comes highly recommended."

The battleship would soon make short work of this misogynist pig. She was developing a new-found respect for the Battleship McCluskey.

"Thanks for coming in guys. I appreciate you going and fetching the Bobbsey twins."

"They weren't very keen on helping us with our enquiries, Ma'am."

"Did you get hurt, Jason?"

"Not a scratch. Everything is intact and working as it should."

"You've a choice. You can either go home or come and listen to gossip in the pub with us."

Peter opted for home and his slippers. The boys opted for a night out.

"It's not a night out. It's work. One drink and keep your eyes and ears open."

"Got it, Ma'am. Best behaviour. No alcohol," said Roy.

"Come on, let's go get bladdered."

"Jason, I'm warning you."

Laughing they rushed out the door. Shona drove them to the Perth Road. The lads could drink and get a taxi home. She'd be on sparkling mineral water. If the scruffy Rabbie stocked it, that was. Otherwise she'd be swigging back coke. Still, it would leave her with a clear head to speak to Hui Chao.

Not always one to pray, she did that night. Prayed her best prayers that the guru would be in attendance and she wouldn't have to go and pin him down. She had a feeling if anyone could answer her questions it would be him. Being a con man meant you soaked up information like a sponge. Being a spiritual advisor meant people told you everything.

58

It was not to be.

They hadn't set foot out the door before the desk sergeant caught them. "Ma'am, there's someone wants to speak to you."

"Can't it wait until tomorrow?"

"I tried that. She said no. To be honest she looks terrified. I think if she leaves she'll flee and we'll never see her again."

She sighed. "Boys, back upstairs. I've another interview to conduct. Jason, you can do it with me."

"How can I help you, Miss…?"

"Lorimer. Frankie Lorimer. Call me Frankie."

"What can I do for you Frankie?"

"I didn't know what to do. I didn't want to come. Maybe I should go." She stood up.

"You're safe here you can tell me anything."

"I wouldn't have come but when she was found…"

"When who was found?" Shona's voice was gentle. What she wanted to do was scream.

"Meredith Crayford."

Shona was now listening intently, all thoughts of the pub gone. "You knew Meredith?"

"I was her nanny."

"It was you who was with the children the night she disappeared?"

"Yes. It was horrible for weeks after that. I didn't want to say anything. I was scared."

"About what?" The girl was quiet. Shona could see conflicting emotions flicker through her eyes.

"About what, Frankie?" she said softly.

"Liam Crayford abused her."

Shona bit back a cheer. At last something to move forward on.

"In what way?"

"He beat her. He was also verbally abusive. She had a dreadful life. That was the first night she was brave enough to go out on her own."

"Did you say anything at the time?"

"No. I knew deep in my soul she was dead. I was terrified he would kill me as well."

The young woman burst into tears. "I'm sorry. I'm really sorry. I should have said something. I know I should have said something. It's been so hard."

By rights the woman should be charged with withholding information. In practice Shona didn't have the heart. It wouldn't go anywhere in court and she would be pulled apart as a witness if it went that far.

"Liam was at work that night," said Shona. "How did he seem when he got in?"

"He seemed agitated. I thought he'd been snorting cocaine or something."

"Please could you give a statement to my constable? Thank you for coming forward. We will certainly be looking into this."

Shona popped along to the Chief's office. He and the big boss were long gone. She pulled out her mobile and rang the Chief. The big boss was staying overnight with him. She outlined the situation. She was passed on to the Chief Constable who said he would discuss it with Thomas and get back to her. This left her tapping her heels until the phone rang. Their advice was to leave it until the morning.

"He's not going to flee into the night after all this time. He probably thinks he's got away with it. Pull him in for an interview when there's someone to look after the kids". She hung up and threw her mobile into her handbag.

Once the interview was completed they made another break for the pub. This time they made it.

59

Shona ordered two pints of bitter, a lager, a coke and three sausage rolls. The boys went to mix with the film crew and she went to speak to Hui Chao. He looked startled to see her but moved up at her request that she join him.

"How's life as a counsellor and spiritual guru?"

"Stop making a fool of me."

"I'm not. I'm genuinely trying to be nice."

"It's good. Have you finished with my Dictaphone yet?"

"I'm sorry, it's evidence until further notice."

"I can't afford to buy a new one."

"When you can afford it remember to tell people you're recording their conversation. It's illegal otherwise."

Someone tried to join them at the table but she glared at them. "We're having a private conversation here, pal."

"It's a pub. I can sit where I like."

She rammed her ID card on to his nose. "Do one."

The drunk ambled off and left them to it. Not a soul took any notice of the altercation. Apart from her three, of course, who were keeping a wary eye on her. *Aww, bless.*

"Right I'm going to ask you questions and you're going to answer them as though we're having a chat. I'm sure you know someone else has been killed."

He nodded and Shona laughed and slapped his arm.

"You could be next given the amount you know."

His face turned white which was some feat given his ethnic background and the colour of his skin.

He nodded again.

"For heaven's sake say something, man. And smile

occasionally. We're meant to be having a conversation."

He was a quick learner. A smile appeared on his lips. "Of course you can talk to me, my daughter."

Shona was getting a bit fed up of all the false platitudes. However, she rolled with it. At least he was playing along.

"What would you like to say? I can help you."

She leaned in and lowered her voice. "What's the skinny with Xavier and Clarissa?"

"They hate each other. Have done for years."

"Do you know why? Have they been competing for jobs or something?"

"That's part of it. They were always fighting over directing gigs. A right fiery pair. Half the time they were going at it hammer and tongs."

"You said part of it. What's the other part?"

"There's a rumour going around that he had an affair with her mother."

"From what I've heard in the past few days I wouldn't say that was unusual."

"It's not. What is unusual is that Clarissa's mother was of a nervous disposition. Actually she was completely barmy. She committed suicide when Xavier dumped her."

Shona said in a fairly loud voice, "Thank you Hui Chao, you've really helped me come to terms with my feelings. I'm glad we spoke."

The Glaswegian con man winked at her and smiled. She owed him one.

"What's your poison? I'll get you one."

"Orange juice. Buddhists don't drink."

"You really are a Buddhist?" Her voice squeaked with amazement.

"I really am."

The bar was packed so they took themselves off to one with less custom. They found a table in the corner that was quiet and private. Armed with drinks they had a debrief.

"They're all bricking it in that film company. They're wondering who's going to be next," said Roy.

"Several of them are thinking of ditching it and getting out of the way. The only thing keeping them here is us lot asking them to stay," added Jason.

This left Iain to get his tuppence ha'penny in. "I think some of them are going to go anyway. More terrified of being murdered than of the police."

"Great, when we've nary a clue who did it."

She updated them on the conversation with the guru. "And to top it all he really is a Buddhist monk."

"So a leopard really can change its spots?" said Roy.

"Finding out about the director's feud doesn't really help us with the investigation. Clarissa wasn't even in Scotland when the initial murders happened."

"She was, Ma'am," said Iain.

"What? How the devil did you find that out?"

"Alex, at the bar, said he hadn't seen her in here since she started the director's gig. She and her partner swigged back champagne like lemonade. Spent a fortune."

"So Clarissa's a suspect?"

"Well done boys but I don't think we can do anything more tonight. I'll see you back at the station bright and breezy in the morning."

60

The weather may have been bright but Shona did not feel particularly breezy. In fact, she felt like a half-shut knife. The warm weather and Shakespeare claiming most of the bed added to her general feeling of exhaustion the next morning. This was going to be a fully-loaded caffeine day.

She carried her coffee in to the office.

"Nina and Abigail." She handed them the file from the previous evening. "Can you read this and get Liam Crayford in for questioning?"

"Sure thing." They sat down and read the file. "Blimey, Ma'am. How come this wasn't picked up when she went missing?"

"To be honest when I went to see him I wouldn't have suspected anything like that. He came across as being quite a nice bloke."

She gave them a brief overview of what had happened in the pub.

"I didn't see that coming," said Abigail.

"Me neither. It just goes to show you can't discount anything."

"Roy, I want to know if Clarissa Claris-Beauchamp has any links to America. See if she's been there recently?"

"Legal or slightly dodgy for the search?"

"This is full-blown dodgy time. Do whatever you have to. I'll square it with the bosses."

Shona's heart was beating much more rapidly than it should have been. This didn't mean they'd found their killer. *What possible motivation would she have to sabotage her own movie. Actually it wasn't her movie to begin with. It was Xavier's. Maybe this was payback time.*

She ran this past Peter.

"It's pretty elaborate for payback, Ma'am. Do you no' think it's a wee bittie excessive?"

"I've come to the conclusion anyone involved in the film industry is a raving egomaniac. They can't see anything from anywhere other than their own viewpoint. It would make perfect sense to her."

An anxious, nail-biting, arm-chewing hour later, Roy came and found her. "She most certainly does have contacts in America. She's involved in a Broadway play. Been over there three times in the last year."

"Bingo. So she could have imported the baseball bats." She did a little jig.

She was on her way to see the Chief when Abigail and Nina found her.

"Liam insisted he had an alibi for that night. He was at work in a meeting. One of his work colleagues is on his way in. Should be about five minutes as the office is close by."

"Nice one. Keep me updated."

The Chief Constable was nowhere to be seen. The Chief looked exhausted. "Are you all right, Sir?"

"Yes. Too many late nights. What do you want?"

"I know how you feel, Sir."

She gave him a succinct update as to where they were now and how everything was pointing to Clarissa perhaps being the killer. "Do we have enough for an arrest?"

He thought for a moment. "Not quite yet. Dig around a bit more."

She brought him up to date with what was

happening with Liam Crayford. "If we can break his alibi then we have a case."

"Keep me informed, Inspector. That will be all."

His bent head was dismissive. They were back to normal then.

61

Shona asked Peter to go down to the film set with her. Given the perilous state of Peter's feet the day before, they drove down. Peter pulled a packet of toffees from his pocket and offered her one. They chewed in companionable silence until they reached the Discovery.

Clarissa was nowhere to be seen. Seemingly she'd gone off to buy her partner a birthday present and would be gone about an hour. Shona asked if she could use Clarissa's van to do some more interviews.

"Please do, Inspector, I shall join you in a few moments. I just need to get this make-up off."

They went in to the van and helped themselves to coffee. Peter was more of a tea drinker but there was only Earl Grey.

"I'm not drinking that poncey stuff."

"I've never been in a van like this. I'm going to have a look around."

"You can't do that. We've not got a warrant."

"Not for evidence. I just want to see what the bedroom and bathroom are like."

The bathroom was beautiful with an elegant shower. The bedroom was huge for a camper van. It had a circular bed which had....

Shona stood stock still and stared. It had a long thick cloak lying over the top of it. A bit like the one Sherlock Holmes would wear. Hadn't one of the witnesses said something about someone in a long cloak?

There were a row of wigs on the dresser. All multi-coloured.

Shona shot out of the room. She'd just sat down when Felix appeared.

"Felix, thank you for coming to talk to us. I just need to know a few more things?"

"Of course, ask away."

"When was Della last in the United States?"

"Some years ago, before her mother died. Yes, definitely before then."

"Did she bring back baseball bats as presents?"

"I'm afraid I don't know."

How does he not know I'm talking a load of crap?

Peter certainly did. He had a puzzled look on his face.

"That's been helpful thank you." She got up to leave. "Oh, I just remembered. I wanted to ask Clarissa where she got her hair dyed. It's gorgeous."

"It's not dyed, dear lady. She wears wigs. Her own hair is short and grey. Not nearly flamboyant enough for her."

"Never. She had me fooled. By the way, what sort of car does she drive? I bet it's something flamboyant."

"Vintage Bentley."

"I wouldn't have put her down as the vintage Bentley type. I'd have guessed a Porsche or something sporty."

"Looks can be deceiving. She's more of the staid type when it comes to driving."

"I wouldn't mind a vintage Bentley myself."

"Too slow for me."

She briefed Peter on the way back to the station. They stopped off at the Sheriff's office to get a search warrant. The Sheriff took in her urgent demeanour and gave her it straight away.

"Don't do anything daft, Shona. This woman sounds like she's got violence written into her DNA."

"I agree, Sir. She's also got murder written on her heart."

62

The Chief was not amused. "You did what? You know that is trespass. Also the evidence you got is inadmissible in court."

"Sir, I was told to use the van. I was looking for the bathroom and ended up in the wrong place."

"Why do I not believe you, Shona?"

"I'm sure I have no clue."

"By the way, Liam's alibi held up. We had to let him go."

"So he's got away with murder."

"We don't know that. However, if he did murder his wife we will get him one day."

"Thank you Sir. One last request."

"The answer is no."

"You don't know what I was going to say."

"I do. You will not be signing out guns. It is too enclosed down there and too public."

"But, Sir."

"That is my final word on the matter. Do your job and arrest the woman without injury, guns or mayhem."

"Of course, Sir."

She went to find Iain.

"Did you ever work out what make of car made that tyre mark up at Camperdown Park?"

"Yeh. Funny thing. It was a Bentley. You don't see many of those around here."

Bingo. They had themselves a killer.

Shona got her team together along with a few willing PCs that she'd begged off Steve. The pizza bribe had obviously worked as he handed them over, if not graciously, at least without complaining.

"This woman is dangerous. She is obviously strong. In the way of weapons we know she has used at least one knife. She also has access to an undisclosed number of baseball bats."

"Are we signing out weapons?" Jason was doing his best imitation of Charlie the puppy.

"No. Not under any circumstances. There are too many members of the public and this is broad daylight."

The boys had a hangdog look. This was the best part of being in her team as far as they were concerned.

"I mean it. Jason, if I see you with any weapon your mate has given you, you will be thrown off the force. Do not test me on this."

"Yes, Ma'am."

"Constables, thanks for joining us. You will be providing a guard around the periphery of the film set. We will be going in."

"Yes, Ma'am."

"My team. Space will be tight in there. Make sure no one gets hurt."

They nodded.

"Let's go."

63

The squad cars dropped them off at the front of the film set. Nina and Abigail went in to Discovery Point to tell the staff to stay in their offices. The PCs secured the area and asked bystanders to leave. The rest of them rushed into the film set.

Cast and crew scattered as they entered. Felix saw them and said, "What's going on?"

"I have a search warrant to search Clarissa's van." She showed it to him.

She moved over to the van and knocked on the door.

Clarissa opened it. This was the real Clarissa without the wig. She took one look and the door slammed shut.

"Open the door."

No response.

"Get a battering ram."

Jason hurtled off towards the squad cars. He returned with the battering ram and a PC.

"Police. Open the door."

Nothing.

"Knock it in."

They were preparing to do this when Clarissa appeared. She now had on a green and purple wig and had a baseball bat in her hand.

Jason and the PC prepared to rush forward and knock her over.

Before they could move Clarissa swung the bat around her head and in the direction of the two officers. As they took the first step the bat made contact with Jason's hand. Even over the hubbub a sickening crunch could be heard. Jason screamed and dropped the battering ram. It landed on the PC's foot.

"Everyone get back."

Clarissa was running towards them swinging the bat. It missed Shona's head by a whisker. She could feel the breeze as it whizzed past her ear.

"Everyone out of the way. Don't put yourself in danger."

Clarissa was running towards the exit the bat still swinging. Shona bolted after her with Peter and Roy in hot pursuit. Iain brought up the rear.

She was thanking her lucky stars that the PCs had got any members of the public well back. Shona was wishing she had a gun about her person. She could just about do with one now. The Chief was right though. Far too many people around.

Clarissa was heading for her car, which was parked in the Discovery car park. Just as she rounded the bushes to get into the car park she went head over heels and crashed to the ground. She'd tripped over one of Adanna Okafor's elegant legs. One which had been strategically stuck out to aid the police.

The raging Clarissa did not stay lying down for long. She got to her knees and swung the bat which she was still holding. It made contact with Adanna's face and a huge gaping wound appeared. Adanna screamed. Clutched her face and staggered back. The screaming continued.

The sound stopped Clarissa just long enough to give the police the advantage. The bat stopped and Roy grabbed. He yanked hard but couldn't get it out of the woman's grip. However, it allowed Shona and the others to pile on top of Clarissa. The PCs joined in and they managed to get handcuffs on her. Peter wasn't looking too good.

A bit blue about the gills.

"Are you okay?"

"I'm grand, Shona. Just out of breath. I think my wife was right about that diet."

It took four of them to manhandle her, screaming obscenities, into the squad car. Whilst that was happening Shona was ringing an ambulance.

"Bring a first aid kit from one of the cars."

She gently applied a dressing to Adanna's face. "There's an ambulance on its way. Thank you for stepping in like that. We couldn't have made the arrest without you."

Adanna had stopped screaming and was whimpering, tears streaming down her face.

"I've got to go but I'll leave my sergeant with you. She'll stay with you until you are at the hospital." She called Nina over and left her gently soothing Adanna.

64

Shona had never been so glad to see Bell Street in her life. She would never complain about it again. There was a crowd of press and onlookers standing around the station steps.

"Out of the way." She could barely see for camera flashes and the bright sunlight.

"I said get out of the way."

No one could hear her above the bellowing of the prisoner. Suddenly the bellowing stopped and Clarissa went limp. No one could hold her up.

"Get back. Get everyone back and out of here."

The duty sergeant came out, took in the urgency of her voice and got the crowd out of the way. This left a large enough area that Shona could take in what had happened to Clarissa. She was lying on the ground, blood everywhere and her bowels lying on the ground beside her. The light of life was fast fading from her eyes.

"Get an ambulance and wet dressings. Now," shouted Shona.

The reason for the injury was standing right next to them. Xavier Lovelady was covered in Clarissa's blood and had a naval cutlass in his hand.

"You ruined my movie. This was my one work of love and you took it away from me. I hope you rot in hell."

"Roy, get this weapon off him and take him inside."

Xavier was compliant as he handed over the knife and

followed Roy inside. All the fight had gone out of him.

By the time the ambulance arrived it was too late for Clarissa. It was not, however, too late for Peter. As the ambulance arrived he grabbed his chest and fell to his knees.

"Peter, what's wrong?"

Peter's face was grey and his eyes shut.

"We need help over here."

The paramedics rushed over. They felt his pulse and checked for breathing. "He's still alive." They got him on a trolley, attached oxygen, put him in the back of the ambulance and closed the doors.

Shona stood in a pool of blood, watching the ambulance carrying her friend disappear down Bell Street. Would she ever see him again?

WENDY H. JONES

Wendy H. Jones lives in Dundee, Scotland, and her police procedural series featuring Detective Inspector Shona McKenzie, is set in Dundee.

Wendy, who is a committed Christian, has led a varied and adventurous life. Her love for adventure led to her joining the Royal Navy to undertake nurse training. After six years in the Navy she joined the Army where she served as an officer for a further 17 years. This took her all over the world including the Middle East and the Far East. Much of her spare time is now spent travelling around the UK, and lands much further afield.

As well as nursing Wendy also worked for many years in Academia. This led to publication in academic textbooks and journals. Killer's Crew is the fifth book in the Shona McKenzie series.

THE DI SHONA McKENZIE MYSTERIES

Killer's Countdown
Killer's Craft
Killer's Cross
Killer's Cut

FIND OUT MORE

Website: http://www.wendyhjones.com

Full list of links: http://about.me/WendyHJones

Twitter: https://twitter.com/WendyHJones

Photographs of the places mentioned in the book can be found at: http://www.pinterest.com/wjones64/my-dundee/